The Queens Gambit

Shane Reed

The Queens Gambit

Shane Reed

Copyright

Copyright © 2024 by Shane Reed

All rights reserved.

Table of Contents

Chapter 1

Nathaniel "Nate" Everhart stood like a beacon in the dimly lit foyer, his tall frame casting long shadows across the polished floor. Dark hair, peppered with the wisdom of his early forties, fell in a casual disarray that somehow complemented the sharp lines of his jaw. The soft light caught in the silver threads and danced with a life of its own.

"Are you ready?" Amy's voice, rich and confident, broke through his focus.

He turned, eyes settling on his partner in justice. Amelia "Amy" Everhart was stunning, her striking red hair a flame against the backdrop of night, the locks tumbling over her shoulders in an elegant cascade of curls. Her mid-30s graced her with an air of maturity that only enhanced her natural allure.

"Always," Nate replied, his voice carrying that edge of charisma that had talked them out of more tight spots than he cared to count. As he spoke, his fingers danced over the keyboard of his rugged laptop, the screen awash with lines of code—a symphony of digital warfare composed by his deft hands.

His mind raced back to the days of desert sands and military commands, where the stakes were life and death, not just bytes and data. The transition from soldier to cyber-savior hadn't been seamless, but it was necessary. With each keystroke, he remembered why he'd swapped his rifle for routers—justice had a new battlefield, and he was its white-hat knight.

"Any sign of the firewall cracking?" Amy asked, peering over his shoulder.

"Like butter on a hot skillet." Nate couldn't help but smirk at the analogy. His intelligence wasn't just raw IQ; it was a street-smart savvy that could read weakness in any system, human or silicon.

"Good. Once we're in, it's showtime," she said, the corner of her lips quirking up in anticipation.

"Showtime" was their shorthand for the moment when all their plans converged, when the con they meticulously crafted came to life. It was the crescendo of their elaborate symphony, the rush that kept them chasing after the next big score—the one that would set another wrong to right.

"Remember, we're doing this for the Carters," Nate muttered to himself, aligning his resolve with the faces of the family they were fighting for. They had been fleeced by a corporate shark, and Nate felt each injustice as if it were carved into his own skin. Empathy was his compass, guiding him through the gray areas of law and morality.

"Empathy is what makes you good at this," Amy had once told him, and he held onto that. It was the balance to his wife's razor-sharp instincts, her journalist's eye that missed nothing—not even the flicker of doubt that sometimes clouded his gaze.

"Empathy and a damn fine ability to break through any security system," Nate added under his breath.

"Damn fine doesn't begin to cover it," Amy agreed, stepping back to let him work his magic.

The dance of their partnership was intricate, a pas de deux of skill and instinct. Where he pushed, she pulled. When he dove headfirst into the abyss of ones and zeroes, she anchored him to reality with her quick wit and quicker reflexes.

"Almost there..." Nate's whisper was barely audible, a prayer to the gods of cyberspace.

"Then hurry up, we don't have all night," Amy teased, though her eyes betrayed the gravity of their mission. Every second counted, every move had to be precise. There was no room for error—not when lives and livelihoods were on the line.

With a final flourish, Nate breached the last barrier, the firewall crumbling beneath his onslaught. "We're in."

"Let's make it count." Amy's hand found his shoulder, a silent vow passing between them. Together, they were unstoppable—an A-Team for the digital age, dedicated to righting the countless wrongs that slipped through society's cracks.

"Let's," Nate agreed, closing his laptop with a snap. The game was afoot, and Nate and Amy Everhart were ready to play.

Amy Everhart's eyes were the kind that missed nothing—a journalist's eyes, honed sharp as a scalpel. She scanned the scene before her, every detail a piece of the puzzle they'd been assembling for months. The subtle shift in the bodyguard's stance, the nervous flicker of an accountant's gaze; each was a thread in the tapestry of corruption they aimed to unravel.

"See that, Nate?" Amy murmured, her voice low and steady. "Three o'clock. That's our mark."

"Got him," Nate replied without looking up from the laptop where he was cross-referencing names and faces. His fingers flew across the screen with practiced ease.

"Good. Keep tabs on his movements." Her focus never wavered, red hair like a flame in the dim light—a beacon of their intent. "I'll circle back after I chat with our friend from the zoning commission."

"Be careful," he said, but he knew she didn't need the warning. Caution was woven into the fabric of her being, just as much as her relentless drive for justice.

"Always am," she shot back with a confidence that matched her stride as she moved away, weaving through the crowd with purpose. With each step, she catalogued everything: the too-loud laughter at the bar, the hushed deals cloaked in pleasantries, the hum of greed that buzzed beneath the surface.

As Amy approached her target, Nate watched through a sea of oblivious partygoers. Their operation was like clockwork, their trust in each other absolute. He admired her ability to slip into any role, to extract information as easily as breathing. She had a way of making people want to tell her their secrets—a skill that made her invaluable.

"Mr. Robertson," Amy greeted the zoning official with a smile that was all charm and no warmth. "Mind if I steal a moment?"

"Ms. Everhart, isn't it?" Robertson's oily grin didn't reach his eyes. "I'm surprised to see you here."

"Surprised, but not displeased, I hope," she replied, tilting her head slightly, letting him think he had the upper hand.

"Never displeased to speak with a beautiful woman," he said, leaning in a bit too close.

"Then let's talk business." Amy's tone shifted, a subtle hardening around the edges, and Nate could see the moment Robertson realized he was not in control of this dance.

"Of course," he conceded, taking a gulp of his drink.

Nate's attention returned to his own device, pulling up blueprints and schematics, seeking the vulnerabilities they would exploit later. His mind raced with possibilities, strategies unfolding like a map before him. He could hear Amy's voice, even from across the room, pressing for the truth hidden behind numbers and niceties.

"Remember, we're doing this for the Davids against the Goliaths," Nate reminded himself, the thought a steady drumbeat in his heart. As Amy worked her magic, drawing out the confession they needed, Nate prepared for the next phase. Together, they were more than partners—they were a force of nature, a storm against the strongholds of the untouchable.

"Got what we need," Amy's voice tickled his earpiece moments later.

"Meet you at the exit in two," Nate confirmed, already on the move.

"Copy that."

Their escape was as smooth as their entrance, shadows blending into shadows. Outside, under the cover of night, Amy's green eyes met his with a fire that spoke of victories yet to come.

"Another step closer," she said, her conviction a tangible thing between them.

"Another step toward justice," Nate agreed, feeling the adrenaline begin to ebb. Tomorrow, they'd face new challenges, but tonight, they'd struck another blow for those who couldn't fight for themselves. And that was all that mattered.

Nate's fingers flew across the keyboard, each tap a step toward justice. The screen glowed, a beacon in the dim hotel room. Amy paced behind him, her silence as loud as an alarm bell.

"Any minute now," she muttered, her voice tight with anticipation.

"Almost there." Nate's reply was curt, his focus unbreakable.

They were on the trail of a corporate shark, one who preyed on the pensions of the elderly, the savings of the hardworking. Nate felt it in his core, the wrongness of it all. His past—a uniform, a creed, a promise to protect—it all funneled into this moment.

"Got it!" He exhaled sharply. The firewall crumbled under his assault. Numbers and ledgers bared before them, digital secrets no longer whispered.

"Show me," Amy demanded.

He angled the screen her way. Her eyes darted across the data, a predator zeroing in on the lie. "Bingo. There's the discrepancy."

"Leaking it to the press?"

"Like a sieve." She grinned, but her eyes were steel.

Nate stood, stretching out the tension. They had to move quickly, cover their tracks. Every second counted. He wiped the laptop clean with practiced ease, a ghost leaving no trace.

"Remember Mrs. Peterson?" he asked, his voice softer now. The woman with trembling hands and eyes too tired from crying. "This is for her. For all the Mrs. Petersons."

Amy nodded, her red hair a fiery banner in the fight.

They slipped into the night, two avengers cloaked in the anonymity of darkness. Nate's heart hammered, not from fear, but from a deep-seated need to balance the scales. Injustice had its enemies, and they were relentless.

"Tomorrow, they wake up to a storm," Amy said, her breath visible in the chilled air.

"Let it rain," Nate agreed, the empathy carved into his soul by years of service now his guiding light.

The air was biting, a sharp reminder of the stakes at play. Amy's breath came out in frosty puffs as she and Nate huddled against the cold brick wall of an unassuming building that housed the corrupt heart they aimed to expose.

"Three minutes tops," Nate muttered, his eyes scanning the alley for any unwanted company.

"Two," Amy corrected. She didn't have to look; she could feel the pulse of the city, the rhythm of danger. It was her metronome, keeping time with their every move.

"Confident?" He arched an eyebrow, but his voice held an edge of admiration.

"Always," she shot back, her fingers dancing across her tablet, securing them a backdoor out of this mess if things went south. "You?"

"Riding on your coattails."

"Damn right." A smirk danced on her lips, but there was no humor in her gaze—only razor-sharp focus.

Nate's phone buzzed—a silent alarm. Time ticked by mercilessly. They were a whisper away from blowing the roof off the exploitation ring that had dug its claws into the city's underbelly.

"Move," Amy commanded, not a second wasted on doubt. Her red hair swung like a war flag as she led the charge down the dark corridor. Her boots clicked against the concrete—steady, determined.

They reached the door. Locked. Of course.

"Plan?" Nate asked, ready to follow her lead.

"Watch." She knelt, picking the lock with a deftness that belied the urgency thrumming through her veins.

"Your dad would be proud," he murmured, the thought surfacing unbidden, a tribute to the man who had taught her so much.

"Let's make sure of it," she said, pushing the door open.

Inside, they were met with a labyrinth of deceit, files stacked like bricks in a wall meant to keep truth at bay. Amy's mind raced. She catalogued the room in seconds—exit points, potential threats, evidence ripe for the taking.

"Cameras," Nate whispered, tension lining his words.

"Got it." She was already on it, a small device in hand that looped the footage—a harmless loop of empty rooms on repeat.

"Seamless," Nate said, a hint of awe in his voice as they moved deeper into the den of lies.

"Focus," Amy snapped, not unkindly. There was no room for error, not when they were so close to vindicating the voiceless, the victims who had placed their trust in them.

"Here." Nate pointed to a safe, tucked away beneath the weight of corruption.

"Can you—" He started, but Amy was already there, stethoscope in ear, dialing in on the safe's secrets with a precision that spoke of years honed on the frontline of investigative journalism.

"Open," she announced, the click of the lock slicing through the silence.

"Brilliant," Nate breathed out, admiration lacing every syllable.

"Let's make it count." Her hands shook, but not from fear. No, it was anticipation—a hunger to right the wrongs that had festered too long in the shadows.

They rifled through the contents, documenting everything with swift, practiced motions. Each file, each piece of evidence, was a step toward justice.

"Time?" Amy's voice was steady, even as her heart raced.

"Minute left," Nate replied, checking his watch. The countdown was relentless.

"Out," she said, the word a bullet shot into the night. They retraced their steps, leaving nothing disturbed, invisible as the wind.

"Nearly there," Nate said once they were outside, the promise of dawn on the horizon.

"Justice doesn't sleep," Amy replied, her thoughts a whirlwind of what was to come.

"Neither do we," Nate confirmed, determination etched into every line of his face.

"Let's bring the storm," she said, and together, they disappeared into the breaking day, a force to be reckoned with.

***

As the early morning light cut through the alley's grime, Nate Everhart's fingers danced across the keyboard of a rugged laptop balanced precariously on a stack of shipping pallets. His eyes, sharp and calculating, flicked between lines of code cascading down the screen and the bustling street beyond their makeshift outpost.

"Traffic cameras are looped," he said with clinical precision, his voice a low rumble. "You're invisible."

"Check," Amy replied, her gaze locked onto the tablet in her hands that mirrored the security feeds Nate had infiltrated. Her red hair was pulled back in a functional ponytail, revealing the determined set of her jaw.

"Power grid?" she asked, without looking up, her fingers swiping through screens with practiced ease.

"Under our control. Blackout in three... two... one." Nate hit 'Enter', plunging a block into darkness, save for the ghostly glow of emergency lights.

"Go time," Amy whispered to herself, the thrill of the hunt sparking behind her sea-green eyes. She slipped from their hideout, a shadow dressed in black, her movements a silent promise of swift justice.

Nate watched her go through the laptop's camera feed, admiration threading through his concern. In another life, he'd have been content just causing a little chaos; now, with Amy, they were a tempest tearing through the city's underbelly.

"Left at the next intersection," he instructed, his voice a lifeline as Amy navigated the maze of alleys.

"Got it," she breathed, her response more felt than heard. He could almost picture her smirk, the one that said she loved this dance as much as he did.

"Two guards ahead. Distract or disable?" Nate queried, ready to deploy a dozen different plans.

"Disable. I've got this," Amy retorted, a hint of mischief in her tone. Moments later, the telltale sounds of incapacitated guards filtered through the comms. Quick, efficient, no-nonsense—as always.

"Nice work," Nate couldn't help grinning. "Four minutes until systems reboot. We need what we came for."

"Understood," Amy confirmed, her words clipped as she approached the target location—a nondescript door, hiding secrets meant for daylight's scorn.

"Ready for the override," Nate announced, his fingers poised.

"Synced," Amy aligned the sequence Nate sent through her own device. The lock clicked open, an invitation to expose the truth hidden within.

"Inside," she confirmed, sweeping the room with a methodical eye. She documented, collected, and categorized evidence with the same meticulous attention that once toppled corrupt politicians and corporate moguls.

"Three minutes," Nate warned, his own heartbeat syncing with the countdown.

"Almost done here," Amy reassured, her thoughts laser-focused on the mission. They didn't have time for doubt—not when every second could mean salvation or ruin for those counting on them.

"Time to move," Nate urged, but there was confidence in his voice. Confidence in her.

"Exiting," Amy said, her silhouette reemerging into the faint dawn light, every step measured and deliberate.

"Safe and sound," Nate breathed out, relief mixing with pride as he closed the laptop. Together, they walked away from the scene, indistinguishable from the early risers beginning their day.

"Clean as a whistle," Amy quipped, her adrenaline-fueled grin infectious.

"Like clockwork," Nate agreed, their camaraderie a testament to the bond forged in the fires of their shared cause.

"Next step?" Amy inquired, her mind already racing ahead.

"Next step," Nate echoed, his eyes on the horizon, where justice waited for those with the courage to chase it.

The early morning sun cast long, angular shadows across the worn-out facade of the community center, a stark contrast to the new day dawning. Inside, huddled masses of hopeful faces turned as the door creaked open, revealing Nate and Amy, their silhouettes brimming with promise.

"Everyone," Nate's voice resonated through the anxious space, "you can rest easy now." His tone carried the weight of countless sleepless nights spent in pursuit of justice for these people.

Amy moved among them, her gaze meeting each pair of eyes, seeing the flickers of hope rekindling. "We've secured the evidence," she said, her voice a soothing balm to their frayed nerves. "The ones who did this to you—they'll face the consequences."

A murmur rippled through the crowd, a mixture of relief and disbelief. Nate watched, his chest tightening at the sight of tears welling up, spilling over—years of injustice being washed away by the simple act of being heard. He felt it, that familiar surge of empathy, fueling his resolve.

"Your fight is our fight," he declared, words etched with sincerity born from his own scars.

Amy's hand found his, a silent acknowledgment of the invisible thread that connected them to this moment, to these people. They had become more than just defenders; they were avengers in the eyes of those who had been wronged.

"Tell us what happens next?" An elderly man stepped forward, his question piercing the newfound calm.

"Next," Amy responded, her mind already analyzing the moves ahead, "we take this fight to the steps of the courthouse. We don't stop until everyone responsible is held accountable."

Nate nodded, affirming her statement. "And we won't back down. We've never backed down."

"Thank you," a young woman whispered, clutching Amy's hand. "For not giving up on us."

As they exited the center, the couple shared a look—a silent conversation passing between them. Their path was clear, the stakes higher than ever. With every stride, they left an impression in the dust, a testament to their relentless pursuit of justice.

"Ready for round two?" Nate asked, his focus locked on the road ahead.

"Always," Amy fired back, her determination fierce as ever.

Nate and Amy Everhart. Marching toward an uncertain future where the only guarantee was their unyielding spirit.

Chapter 2

The sharp ping of Nate's encrypted cellphone cut through the stillness of their home office—a signal that never failed to set his pulse racing. He glanced at Amy, who paused mid-sentence, her finger hovering over the keyboard, red curls cascading like a fiery waterfall as she turned towards him.

"Got something?" she asked, her voice tight with anticipation.

Nate swiped the screen, and his eyes narrowed as he read the message. "Tip's come in. It's the local theater group—the one gearing up for the 'Priscilla, Queen of the Desert' spinoff. Multiple identity thefts among the cast and crew."

"Identity thefts?" Amy repeated, alarm sharpening her emerald eyes. She was instantly on her feet, leaning over his shoulder to glimpse the mysterious text. "How many are we talking?"

"Details are murky, but it's bad enough to make its way to us." Nate's fingers flew over the keys, already tracing digital footprints even as he spoke. "Whoever's behind this knows what they're doing. They're picking off the thespians one by one."

"Thespians? Nate, this isn't Shakespeare," Amy quipped, though her humor couldn't mask the gravity in her voice. "We're talking about a local drag show. But these people have lives off-stage—careers, families. If someone's stealing their identities..."

"Then their world is about to become a stage for something much darker than they signed up for," Nate finished grimly. As an ex-military man who'd seen more than his share of underhanded tactics, he understood all too well the chaos that could ensue from such exploitation.

"Credit lines maxed out, bank accounts drained, reputations ruined," Amy muttered, pacing now, her investigative instincts kicking in. The thought of innocent dreams being shattered by some faceless criminal lit a fire in her that matched the color of her hair.

"Exactly. And if the thief has access to their personal information, what's stopping them from going further?" Nate's thoughts raced, images flashing of the potential devastation: homes invaded, lives upended, futures destroyed.

"Nothing," Amy said with conviction. "We have to move quickly, Nate. These people are artists, not warriors. They're unprepared for this kind of battle."

He nodded, aware that the clock was ticking—for the victims and for them. "We'll need to get close. Blend in without drawing suspicion. The closer we are, the quicker we can flush out the perpetrator."

"Time to brush up on our musical theater, then." A mischievous glint sparked in Amy's eyes, despite the seriousness of the situation.

"Guess it's time to find out how good you look in sequins, Mrs. Everhart," Nate shot back, his own brand of dark humor surfacing despite the urgency.

"Better than you, Mr. Everhart," she retorted with a smirk, already mentally cataloging each step they needed to take.

They both knew the stakes were high. Someone was playing a dangerous game with people's lives, and it was up to Nate and Amy to bring down the curtain on the scheme.

The moment the door closed behind them, the air in their cramped office seemed to crackle with electricity. Nate leaned against the worn wooden desk that had seen better days, a grin spreading across his face, mirroring Amy's own elation. They were on the scent of something big, and the thrill of the chase was a familiar intoxicant.

"Imagine," Nate began, the excitement evident in his voice as he straightened, "someone using the chaos of costume changes and stage makeup to hide in plain sight."

"Right under their noses," Amy chimed in, her eyes alight with the spark of the hunt. She paced the room, two steps forward, two steps back, like a caged tiger ready to pounce. "It's clever, I'll give them that."

"Too clever by half," Nate countered, his brain already churning through scenarios. He tapped a finger on his temple, where the gears of strategy were spinning at full speed. "We need to be even more cunning."

Amy stopped her pacing, turned, and planted her hands on the desk, leaning towards Nate. Her red hair fell like a fiery curtain, framing her determined expression. "So, how do we worm our way into their world without setting off any alarms?"

"Simple," Nate said with a conspiratorial smirk. "We make ourselves indispensable."

"Ah, the old 'hide in plain sight' technique." Amy's lips curled into a smile that was all sharp edges and challenge. "I've always fancied myself a bit of an actress."

"Good thing you married a man who appreciates the fine arts," Nate quipped, pushing off the desk to join her in the strategizing dance. "But this isn't just about acting. We need intel, hard facts. And for that, we need to be welcomed inside their circle."

"Then let's craft our characters," Amy suggested, her mind racing ahead. "The new tech enthusiasts? Or perhaps a pair of traveling theater buffs looking to volunteer?"

"Both good covers," Nate agreed, nodding thoughtfully. "But let's not rush the audition. We need to know the players before we can decide on our roles. Who's vulnerable, who's hiding something..."

"Who's pulling the strings," Amy finished for him. It wasn't just a question of what role they would play but how they would play it. The precise angle of approach could mean the difference between success and catastrophic failure.

"Exactly." Nate circled round the desk and booted up their computer, the screen bathing his features in a ghostly glow. "Time for some recon. Let's see who these thespians really are when they're not under the spotlight."

"Lead the way, Sherlock," Amy said, the curl of her lip betraying her anticipation. As Nate's fingers flew over the keyboard, she hovered close, watching the names and faces flicker onto the screen. Each one a potential lead. Each one a potential victim.

"Whatever secrets they're hiding," Nate murmured, his focus absolute, "we'll uncover them."

"Then it's showtime," Amy whispered, her gaze locked on the glowing monitor, feeling the adrenaline surge within her. "Let the masquerade begin."

As Nate delved into the digital archives of the theater group, Amy stood sentinel, her thoughts sharp as knives. Together, they would unmask the villain of this production, no matter the cost.

Nate's fingers danced across the keyboard, a silent concerto of clicks and clacks filling the room.

"Find anything juicy?" Amy asked, her voice low, as if the walls themselves might be eavesdropping on their covert operations.

"Juicy's an understatement," Nate replied without looking away from the monitor. "We've got aliases, dummy accounts—a whole smorgasbord of deceit."

Amy leaned over his shoulder, her eyes scanning the information that Nate teased out from the shadows of cyberspace. She felt the familiar thrill of the hunt, the scent of a story worth telling. Her instincts, honed from years of chasing leads and sniffing out lies, tingled with anticipation.

"Keep digging," she urged. "The deeper we go, the dirtier it gets."

They had to be smart about this—no footprints in the digital dust. Nate's hands were steady, his mind sharp as he navigated through encrypted files and private messages. He was a ghost in the machine, his presence undetectable, his touch lighter than air.

"Remember, we can't spook them," Amy said, straightening up and pacing the confined space of their makeshift war room. "If they catch even a whisper of suspicion..."

"They won't." Nate's assurance was as solid as the desk they hunched over. "I've covered our tracks. Tor, VPN, false IP... We're invisible."

She nodded, satisfied. They were a team—a seamless unit functioning on trust and mutual respect. And as much as Nate's prowess with technology kept them one step ahead, it was Amy's gut feeling that often pointed them in the right direction.

"Here," Nate said suddenly, pointing at the screen where a list of names glowed ominously. "These are the ones with access to the group's finances. If anyone's playing puppet master with identities, my bet's on one of these charmers."

"Good," Amy responded crisply, her mind already racing ahead. "Now, let's talk strategy. We need to blend in, become one with the troupe. Flawless personas that don't raise an eyebrow."

"Right," Nate agreed, swiveling in his chair to face her directly. "Our covers have to be airtight. Any slip-up could blow the entire operation."

"Then we'll be perfect," Amy declared, her determination steel-clad. "Perfectly inconspicuous. The new faces eager to help, not cause waves."

"Exactly. Enthusiastic but unremarkable. Helpful but forgettable." Nate rose from his seat, stretching his limbs before mirroring her pacing. His thoughts ticked away like a bomb timer. There was no margin for error—not when the stakes were this high.

"Let's rundown scenarios," Amy suggested. "Every possible interaction, every question we might face. We need to know our stories better than our own lives."

"Agreed." Nate's jaw set firmly. "It's all about control. Keeping the narrative in our hands. If we can do that, we'll find the breach in their armor."

"Then let's get to work," Amy said, her heartbeat a drumroll of readiness. "We don't have much time, and the clock's ticking louder every second."

They circled back to the desk, two predators ready to spring their trap. Their mission was clear, their resolve unshakable. Together, Nate and Amy were unstoppable. And as the night deepened around them, they plotted, planned, and prepared to dive headfirst into the glittering, deceptive world of the theater.

The computer screen cast a bluish glow on Nate's intent face as he scrolled through the digital dossier of headshots and bios, each member of the local theater group unwittingly an open book to his probing cyber gaze. Amy leaned over his shoulder, her red hair brushing against his cheek as she pointed at the screen, "There. That's Marcy Trenton—she's playing on of the leads."

"Divorced twice, recently filed for bankruptcy," Nate muttered, tapping into public records with a few deft keystrokes. "Perfect prey for Identity Theft. But what's the connection? There must be a thread..."

"Patterns, right?" Amy tucked a loose strand behind her ear, eyes darting across the data. "Look for inconsistencies, anything that stands out."

"Here's one: Every victim joined the theater group in the last six months." Nate's fingers flew over the keyboard, highlighting names in red. "Fresh meat for the grinder."

"Anyone from the inside?" Amy's voice was low, a mix of curiosity and cautiousness threading through her words.

"Could be," Nate acknowledged, his mind racing through possibilities as he sifted through membership timelines. "Or an opportunist who's found the perfect hunting ground."

"Risks," Amy began, her tone shifting, "If we're joining this motley crew, there are bound to be landmines. Mistaken identity, recognizing an old mark... or worse, being recognized."

Nate nodded, "We'll need backstories ironclad enough to withstand scrutiny but vague enough not to leave traces." He glanced up at her, "You still good with accents?"

"Like riding a bike," Amy quipped, though her furrowed brow betrayed her concern over keeping their true identities under wraps.

"But our biggest risk is getting too close. Emotional entanglements could cloud our judgment."

"Then we keep it professional. Objective." Nate affirmed, though part of him understood the challenge better than he wished to admit. His mind flickered back to past cases, faces that had haunted him long after justice was served.

"Objective," Amy repeated, though her heart thrummed with empathy for those ensnared in the con. She knew all too well the sting of betrayal, the ache of injustice.

"Let's dive into the production details," Nate suggested, shifting gears as he opened another window filled with rehearsal schedules and set designs. "We need to know 'Priscilla' inside out if we're going to blend in."

"Set building tomorrow night," Amy noted, peering closely at the schedule. "'Volunteers needed.' That's our in. Low profile, just another pair of hands."

"Helpful but forgettable," Nate echoed their earlier mantra. His pulse quickened at the thought of stepping onto the physical stage—their theater of war against deception.

"Exactly," Amy agreed, folding her arms as she took a step back, her mind already rehearsing the role she'd soon play. "We waltz in, smiles ready, and keep our ears open."

"First rule of a con," Nate murmured, half to himself, "listen more than you talk."

"Right," Amy said, nodding sharply. "And the second rule?"

"Stay alive," Nate replied, his lips quirking in a grim smile. "Because in this game, the final curtain could drop at any moment."

Nate's fingers danced across the keyboard, the staccato clicking a stark underscore to their racing thoughts. Another victim's profile flickered on the screen; bright-eyed and hopeful, now marred by the shadow of financial ruin.

"Another one today," Nate said, voice taut with urgency. "The thief's getting bolder. Or desperate."

"Either way, we're running out of time." Amy paced behind him, her heels striking the floor like a metronome of impatience. "Innocent dreams are being turned into nightmares. We need to act, fast."

"Agreed." Nate swiveled in his chair, eyes meeting hers. A silent vow passed between them, an unspoken oath to shield the unsuspecting from predators lurking in the limelight.

"Then it's settled." Amy stopped pacing, leaning over Nate's shoulder to scan the list of volunteer roles. "We join the crew. Blend in."

"Undercover enthusiasts?" Nate quirked an eyebrow. He could already feel the thrill of the chase, the adrenaline of subterfuge pumping through his veins.

"Exactly." Amy's lips curved in a smile that didn't quite reach her eyes. "We'll be the most devoted volunteers they've ever seen."

"Time to dust off my hammering skills," Nate mused aloud, his mind already cataloging the tools they'd need. "And maybe brush up on my show tunes."

"Let's just stick to hammering, Romeo." Amy chuckled, but her gaze was steel. "We can't afford slip-ups."

"Right." Nate stood, stretching his legs, feeling the coiled readiness of a predator. "No room for error. Not with stakes this high."

They moved together, a fluid dance of preparation, gathering the nondescript clothing and gear that would render them invisible yet invaluable to the theater group.

"Keep it simple. Stay sharp," Nate muttered, slipping a compact toolkit into his bag. "That's how we'll spot the cracks in their facade."

"Simple and sharp." Amy nodded, checking her own bag—notebook, pen, mini recorder. Tools of the trade for an investigative journalist. "Just two new faces in the crowd."

"Two new faces with one goal," Nate added, zipping his bag shut with finality. Their reflection in the darkened window showed a couple ready for anything. Ready to dive into the masquerade ball of misdeeds and unmask the villain.

"Let's do this," Amy said, her hand finding Nate's, their grip a testament to their shared resolve.

"Let's," Nate agreed, and together they stepped out into the night, towards the twinkling lights of the local theater, where deception awaited its final act.

***

The night air clung to Nate and Amy with a dampness that seeped into their bones, the kind of cold that could make an unprepared soul shiver. But not them; they were wired tight on adrenaline, hearts steady as drums in anticipation.

"Remember," Nate said, his breath clouding before him as they strode toward the theater's back entrance, "trust is currency. We earn it, we spend it, and we find out who's been bankrupting these people."

"Agreed." Amy's voice was a low murmur, her eyes scanning their surroundings. "We'll start by lending a hand with whatever they need—set design, costumes, lighting. No job too small."

"Keep your friends close," Nate mused, "and your suspects closer." His thumb traced the rim of the toolkit hidden within his bag—a hacker's wand ready to reveal digital secrets.

"Exactly." Amy pulled open the door, holding it for Nate as they slipped inside. The scent of fresh paint and sawdust greeted them, mingling with the faintest hint of stage makeup and anxiety.

"Act one," she whispered, her gaze meeting Nate's. The spark in her eyes wasn't just the reflection of the overhead lights—it was pure determination.

"Let's find our cast of characters," Nate replied, his hand gently pressing against the small of her back, guiding her forward through the maze of props and scaffolding. Each step they took was deliberate, a silent promise to the shadows that they wouldn't leave until every stone was turned.

As they emerged onto the main stage, the hubbub of activity crescendoed around them, a symphony of chaos waiting to be orchestrated. Cast members flitted by, lines being rehearsed with fervent urgency—a perfect cover.

"New volunteers!" Amy announced, her voice carrying over the din. Heads turned, sizing them up with the caution reserved for outsiders. "We heard you might need some extra hands?"

"Perfect timing," a harried director called out, his relief palpable as he waved them over. "We're behind schedule. Can you start with helping sort the costumes?"

"Of course," Nate agreed, rolling up his sleeves. "Where do you need us?"

Amy followed suit, diving into the task with feigned naiveté. Every fold of fabric held potential clues, each name tag a piece of the puzzle they were there to solve. As they worked, they listened, letting the ebb and flow of conversations wash over them, sifting through the banter for nuggets of truth.

"Can you believe it?" a voice drifted over, tinged with worry. "Another credit card declined. It's like someone's got it out for us."

"Focus," Nate reminded himself silently, his fingers nimble as he strung sequins onto a costume. "Every slip, every rumor is a lead." His mind was a steel trap, cataloging voices, faces, and names.

"Stay alert," Amy thought, her own internal monologue a mirror of Nate's. "Someone here is playing a dangerous game." Her instincts were honed from years of chasing leads, and now they screamed that the thief was close, hiding in plain sight.

***

"Stick around," the director said, clapping Nate on the shoulder. "We could use more people like you."

"Thank you, we'd love to," Amy responded, warmth in her smile but steel in her spine. They had breached the first wall, sown the first seeds of trust in this garden of deceit.

As the night deepened, Nate and Amy retreated to a quiet corner backstage, their eyes locking in silent conversation. They were in, embedded within the pulse of the production. Now the real work began.

"Tomorrow," Nate whispered, his words barely reaching Amy over the hum of sewing machines and whispered cues. "We dig."

"Tomorrow," Amy affirmed, her hand squeezing Nate's in a mix of comfort and conspiracy. They had laid the groundwork, infiltrated the ranks. Tomorrow they would unravel the mystery thread by thread.

Chapter 3

The envelope lay innocuously among a stack of mundane mail on the Everharts' polished mahogany table, its cream-colored paper and elegant script a stark anomaly. Nate's fingers traced the gold-embossed emblem of the theater group before slicing it open with a practiced flick. He withdrew the invitation, its weight significant in his hands.

"Looks like we've got our golden ticket," he said, a twinkle in his dark eyes as he handed it to Amy.

"Showtime," she replied, scanning the contents with her sharp gaze. The invitation was simple, yet the undercurrents it carried were anything but. To the untrained eye, it was a call to audition, but Nate and Amy sensed the deeper narrative—a story marred by misfortune they were now part of.

"Shall we meet our cast?" Nate mused, that charismatic smile playing on his lips.

"Let's."

✦✦✦

Their entrance into the theater was nothing short of a well-rehearsed act. Diane Peterson greeted them first, her maternal warmth radiating from her kind blue eyes. "You must be the Everharts," she said, extending a hand. "We're thrilled to have fresh talent."

"Thrilled to be here," Nate replied, his handshake firm yet inviting. Diane spoke of the recent setbacks with a furrowed brow, and Nate listened, empathy evident in his attentive posture.

"Martin, Cynthia, Susan, Robert—meet Nathaniel and Amelia Everhart," Diane announced, gesturing toward the others.

Martin Brown, all muscle and intensity, clasped Nate's hand next. His passion for theater was palpable, a fervor that seemingly left no room for doubt or deception. "Looking forward to seeing what you can do," he said, his voice a deep timbre that commanded attention.

"Likewise," Nate responded, noting Martin's single-minded focus.

Cynthia Davis bounced up to them, her blonde curls dancing with each movement. "Hi!" she chirped, blue eyes sparkling. "Isn't this just the most exciting thing?"

"Absolutely," Amy agreed, mirroring Cynthia's infectious energy. Her journalist's mind cataloged the young actress's every mannerism—the tilt of her head, the openness of her smile—textbook naivety.

"New blood, eh?" Susan Thompson's voice cut through, efficient as her stage management. "Don't get in my way, and we'll get along just fine."

"Wouldn't dream of it," Amy returned smoothly, her eyes catching the brief flicker of insecurity behind Susan's green irises.

Lastly, Robert Johnson approached, his pompadour impeccable, his gaze assessing. "Costumes make the character," he stated, "and I am the maestro of fabric."

"We've heard about your legendary skills," Nate complimented, noting how Robert preened at the praise. His ability to read people suggested an advantage they couldn't ignore.

"First rehearsal is tomorrow," Diane reminded them warmly. "We start promptly."

"Wouldn't miss it," Amy assured her, the edge of determination lining her words.

As they left, Nate's thoughts raced with pieces of the intricate puzzle they'd stepped into. Each member of the theater group was a thread in the tapestry of truth they intended to unravel. And unravel it they would—with precision and charm.

***

The evening air was pregnant with the promise of autumn, the sky a watercolor wash of deepening blues. Nate and Amy walked down an alley flanked by red brick walls, their shadows trailing behind like curious specters eager to join the rehearsal. The scent of damp leaves mingled with the faint aroma of coffee drifting from a nearby café.

"Remember," Nate said, keeping his voice low, "we're here to blend in first. Earn their trust."

"Charm and disarm," Amy replied, her eyes gleaming in the twilight.

They paused before the back entrance of the theater, the heavy door painted a peeling black. Nate's hand hovered over the handle—a momentary bastion against the unknown—before he pushed through into the warm glow beyond.

"Energy, that's key," Amy murmured, slipping off her coat. Her fiery hair cascaded over her shoulders, igniting under the stage lights.

"Enthusiasm sells the lie," Nate agreed, his gaze sweeping across the backstage area where props were scattered like remnants of a dream half-remembered.

The rehearsal space hummed with controlled chaos. Diane Peterson was directing actors with a commanding presence, Martin Brown fiddled with a soundboard, Cynthia Davis practiced lines with fervor, while Susan Thompson coordinated movements with military precision. Robert Johnson stood amidst bolts of fabric, his fingers dancing over textures and colors.

"Let's give them a show," Amy said with a smile, looping her arm through Nate's.

"Right behind you, Red," he answered, and they stepped forward into the fray.

"Ah, our newest recruits!" Diane greeted, clasping her hands together. "Ready to jump in?"

"Absolutely," Nate responded, his tone threaded with excitement. He leaned closer, as if sharing a secret. "We've been buzzing about this all day."

"Great! We'll start with the second act. Positions, everyone!"

Amy nodded enthusiastically, glancing at Nate with a look that said, *This is it*. Together, they took their places among the other actors, the script pages feeling crisp and full of potential in their hands.

"From the top," Diane called out, and the rehearsal began.

Nate threw himself into the character, his lines delivered with a natural ease that belied the nerves firing beneath his skin. His military background had taught him composure under pressure, a skill he now used to weave a believable presence on stage. *Keep them focused on the performance*, he reminded himself, *not the performers*.

Amy was equally committed, her posture radiating a confidence that drew eyes to her every move. She slipped into the role with the finesse of a seasoned investigator, each word and gesture another layer of camouflage.

"Bravo!" Martin exclaimed after a particularly intense scene, clapping his hands. "You two are naturals."

"Thanks, Martin," Amy said, her gratitude sounding genuine even as her mind raced. *Every compliment a step closer.*

"Could have fooled me that you're new to this," Susan added, a hint of respect creeping into her voice.

"Thrilled to be here," Nate replied, locking gazes with her for a moment too long—an acknowledgment of the unspoken game they played.

As the rehearsal moved on, Nate could feel the threads of the group weaving around them, pulling them into the fold. With each line, each blocked movement, they sank deeper into the world of the theater and closer to the heart of the mystery that lay within.

"Let's take five," Diane called out, and the intensity of the room deflated into relaxed chatter.

"Seems we're off to a good start," Amy whispered to Nate as they retreated to a quiet corner.

"Too soon to tell," he cautioned, but the twinkle in his eye betrayed his optimism. *Tonight, we perform. Tomorrow, we investigate.* Their mission was only beginning, and the truth was waiting in the wings.

The clamor of scattered scripts and shuffled feet filled the rehearsal space as Nate leaned in towards the director's chair, his suggestion cutting through the din. "Diane, what if we reposition the balcony scene to stage left? It might give it a more secretive ambiance."

Diane Peterson, her silver bob reflecting the harsh rehearsal lights, tapped her chin thoughtfully. "Interesting point," she murmured. Amy, perched on the edge of the stage, watched the group absorb Nate's input, her keen gaze catching the flicker of irritation in Martin Brown's eyes.

"Or," Amy chimed in, her voice silk over steel, "we could introduce a silhouette effect with the lighting during the revelation scene. It'll add a layer of suspense."

"Silhouettes?" Robert Johnson scoffed from behind a canvas backdrop, his skepticism a tangible thing. "Sounds like an amateur hour trick to me."

Nate's posture remained relaxed, but his mind was a live wire, noting the resistance. He met Robert's challenge with a disarming grin. "Maybe so, but think of the drama it could create. The audience loves a bit of spectacle, right?"

"Let's just stick to the basics; we don't need newbies coming in and changing everything," Susan Thompson said, her arms crossed as she appraised them from the wings. Her narrowed eyes were a clear warning—territory was being marked.

"Basics are the foundation," Amy agreed smoothly, not missing a beat, "but sometimes a fresh perspective can breathe life into even the most traditional scenes."

Cynthia Davis, who had been quietly observing the exchange, lifted her script with a thoughtful tilt of her head. "I'm willing to hear them out. What's the harm in trying something new?"

"Exactly," Nate added, his tone suggesting camaraderie rather than confrontation. "Let's run it both ways, see what feels right."

"Fine," Diane conceded, waving a dismissive hand. "But let's not turn this into a circus."

As they resumed rehearsal, Nate and Amy exchanged a quick glance, their silent communication perfected through years of partnership. *Keep pushing, but carefully,* Nate thought, sensing the terrain shift beneath their feet. Amy's nod was imperceptible, but he caught it—their dance of deduction moving in time with the ebb and flow of the theater's dynamics.

"From the top, people!" Diane commanded, and the cast fell into motion, the electric charge of potential change crackling in the air. Nate could feel the weight of scrutiny as they went through the motions, some members of the group warily circling the newcomers like predators sizing up unfamiliar prey.

The musty scent of sawdust and fresh paint hung in the air, a testament to the flurry of activity that had transformed the once-bare stage into a world of its own. Nate, his hands roughened from handling plywood and hammers, was perched atop a ladder, securing a makeshift balcony that would serve as the romantic fulcrum for the play's climactic scene. Below him, Amy was engrossed in stitching sequins onto a resplendent costume, her fingers moving with the precision of a surgeon.

"Careful up there, Nate," Martin called out, eyeing the precarious positioning of the ladder. "We need our lead actor in one piece."

"Appreciate the concern," Nate replied, his voice light, but his mind mapping out the ties between these well-meaning amateurs and the troubles that brought him here. "But I've had my fair share of climbing higher and less stable structures." His military days never felt so distant yet so present.

Amy held up the garment, examining it against the light. "I think this will catch the spotlight just right," she mused aloud, her gaze flickering towards Susan who was arranging props nearby. "What do you think, Susan? Enough glitz for the gala scene?"

Susan approached, squinting at the shimmering fabric. "It's perfect," she confirmed, a smile breaking through. "You have quite the eye, Amy."

"Thanks," Amy said, her smile genuine, even as her journalist's instincts sifted through Susan's words for subtext and hidden stories.

Nate descended the ladder, joining Robert, who was sketching out a lighting plan. "Need a second opinion?" Nate offered, his tone casual. Robert looked up, the lines on his forehead relaxing as he handed over the diagram.

"Could use your tactical insight," Robert admitted. "Scene transitions need to be seamless."

"Let's see what we can rig up," Nate said, his strategic mind already envisioning the flow of illumination like a hacker would data streams, finding the paths of least resistance.

In the costume room, Cynthia was fussing over a rack of dresses, her hands flitting from one hanger to the next. Amy slipped in beside her, a tape measure draped across her shoulders. "The devil's in the details, huh?" Amy quipped, fetching a dress for inspection.

Cynthia chuckled, nervously tucking a strand of hair behind her ear. "You'd be surprised how much a missing button can throw off an entire performance."

"Or how much it can reveal about someone," Amy thought, recalling her father's trial, where the smallest oversight meant everything. Aloud, she simply agreed, "Absolutely."

Rehearsals continued, with Diane directing with a renewed vigor that suggested she was warming up to their presence. During a break, Nate found himself alone with her, both reaching for the coffee pot.

"I would never have taken you for a theatre buff, Nate," Diane remarked, her eyes searching his.

"Life's full of surprises," Nate countered, his smile not reaching his eyes. "Like how a small-town theatre group gets tangled in big-time trouble."

Diane held his gaze a moment longer before pouring her coffee. "We all have our parts to play," she said cryptically, leaving Nate to ponder the double entendre.

***

As the days progressed, each session became more than just preparation for opening night; they were opportunities to weave themselves into the fabric of the group. Nate listened intently to conversations, his mental algorithms sorting through banal chatter for patterns and clues. Amy documented everything, her keen observations forming a narrative that went beyond the script they rehearsed.

"Building sets, sewing costumes, memorizing lines," Amy whispered to Nate during a quiet moment, "it's all part of the act, isn't it? Our most elaborate con."

"Every nail we hammer, every stitch we sew," Nate murmured back, "brings us closer to them, and them to us." Their mission blurred the lines between stage and reality, each day drawing the curtain back just a little more on the truth they sought.

"Alright, places everyone!" Diane's voice rang out, snapping the cast to attention.

The rehearsal unfolded with a renewed sense of unity, the earlier skepticism giving way to a shared purpose. Nate and Amy moved among their fellow actors, their roles now embedded in muscle memory and their intentions hidden behind the guise of passion for the art.

"Break a leg," Susan whispered as they took their positions.

"Let's just hope it's not ours," Amy replied with a wink, the irony of the phrase not lost on either of them as the lights dimmed, signaling the beginning of another scene in their most critical performance yet.

The stage was a maelstrom, a clash of set pieces and prop tables — a test of the Everharts' adaptability. Nate, with his military-honed instincts, navigated the chaos as if it were a complex battlefield, his eyes scanning for the misaligned cue or the misplaced spotlight. Meanwhile, Amy, her investigative senses tingling, cataloged every shift in dynamics, every undercurrent rippling through the group.

"Hey, Nate, the backdrop's mechanism is jammed again," Martin called out, his voice edged with frustration.

Without hesitation, Nate crossed the stage, tools in hand. He assessed the pulley system with the clinical eye of a man who'd once disassembled bombs under pressure. In minutes, he had it gliding smoothly along its track, earning a round of impressed murmurs from the onlookers.

"Man's got a knack for fixing more than just lines," Robert remarked, clapping Nate on the back with a grin.

"Old habits," Nate replied tersely, though the corner of his mouth twitched up in appreciation of the camaraderie that was forming—crucial bonds being forged in the heat of shared challenges.

Amy, meanwhile, found herself amidst a flurry of costume malfunctions. Cynthia's dress had torn along a seam, and Susan's hat had lost its jaunty feather. With nimble fingers, Amy stitched and repaired, her mind working double-time as she noted how the group rallied to support one another in these minor crises.

"Thanks, Amy," Susan said, a sincere warmth in her tone as she took the restored hat. "You're a lifesaver."

"Happy to help," Amy responded, her smile genuine despite the calculating hum of thoughts beneath. These moments of assistance were small threads weaving a stronger connection, a safety net of trust beneath their high-wire act.

During a break, the cast gathered around the newly repaired backdrop, sipping lukewarm coffee and sharing anecdotes from past productions. Nate listened intently, joining in with a humorous tale of an on-stage mishap from his military days that had everyone laughing. The laughter acted as a solvent, dissolving barriers, and he could feel the group's initial skepticism towards him and Amy softening like wax to a flame.

"Never thought I'd see the day when army skills would save a theatre production," Martin chuckled, shaking his head in disbelief.

"Life's full of surprises," Nate quipped, his response light but his gaze sharp, missing nothing.

Amy stood by his side, her laughter mingling with the others', yet her mind remained alert, always seeking, always questioning. She soaked up the stories, the offhand comments, each a potential clue to be stored away for later examination.

"Who knew set-building could bring people together like this?" Robert mused aloud, his expression thoughtful.

"Or tear them apart," Amy added with a playful lilt, her eyes glinting. It was a jest on the surface, but underneath lay the weight of their true purpose here.

"Only if we let it," Diane interjected firmly, giving Amy a pointed look that spoke of an underlying steel. Amy met her gaze evenly, recognizing the challenge and accepting it silently.

As the rehearsal resumed, the Everharts slipped back into their roles, their quick wits and open hearts endearing them to the group. With each line delivered, each scene perfected, they drew closer to unraveling the mystery entwined within the theatre's walls. And with every shared laugh, every exchanged glance of understanding, the line between performance and reality blurred ever so slightly, the stakes of their con growing higher with each passing moment.

The air in the green room was thick with the scent of coffee and fresh paint, a testament to the late nights spent transforming words on a page into living art. In the midst of it all stood Nate, his frame casting a long shadow in the dim light as he leaned against a makeshift table laden with scripts and props.

"Back in the military," Nate began, voice low and inviting, "we had this saying—'embrace the suck.' It's about pushing through when everything goes sideways."

Martin chuckled, flipping through his script. "Sounds like every opening night I've ever had."

"Exactly." Nate's eyes twinkled. "Theatre's not so different from a mission. You've got your team, your objective, and no matter what, the show must go on."

Susan, sitting nearby, her sewing needle paused mid-air, glanced up at him. "You really were in the military?"

"Ten years," Nate replied, allowing a hint of nostalgia to color his tone. "Learned a lot about people... and myself."

Amy watched from the doorway, her silhouette framed by the hallway light. She walked over, perching on the edge of another table, the group's attention shifting to her presence.

"Speaking of learning," she said, picking up a prop feather boa, "my time in investigative journalism taught me that sometimes the smallest details speak the loudest truths."

"Like how Martin always taps his foot before delivering his lines?" Cynthia quipped, earning a round of knowing laughter.

"Or how Diane here can't resist a good costume drama," Amy added, winking at the group's unofficial leader.

Diane smiled, a glimmer of appreciation in her eyes. "Guilty as charged."

"Those little quirks make us who we are," Amy continued, her voice warm with sincerity. "They're the threads that tie a story—or a case—together."

As their camaraderie deepened, the Everharts wove their personal tales into the tapestry of the theatre group. With each shared experience, they fortified their cover, embedding themselves in the fabric of the troupe.

"Last week," Susan confided after a moment, setting her sewing aside, "I found a letter backstage. No name, no signature—just a warning to stop the production." Her voice was a hushed tremor, a ripple of fear disguised as curiosity.

"Any idea who it could be from?" Amy asked, her journalist's instinct surfacing.

"None," Susan admitted. "But things have been off since then. Lights flickering, props misplaced..."

"Sounds like someone's trying to scare us," Martin interjected, his usual joviality edged with concern.

"Could be," Nate mused, his mind racing with possibilities while maintaining a calm exterior. "Or it's a misdirection. Keep us focused on Phantom of the Opera stories while the real threat lurks backstage."

"Either way," Amy said, standing and looping the boa around her neck with a flourish, "we've got a mystery to solve. And I love a good mystery."

A sense of solidarity settled among them, the shared determination to persevere bonding them further. The Everharts, through their genuine engagement and empathy, were no longer outsiders; they were integral to the heartbeat of the group.

Nate met Amy's gaze across the room, a silent communication passing between them. They were closer now, the murmurings of trust beginning to surface. With each revelation, they edged nearer to the truth, the stakes climbing with each confided secret and whispered fear.

"Let's not jump at shadows," Diane said, her voice steady. "We're a family here. And families stick together, right?"

"Right," they echoed, a chorus of resolve amidst the uncertainty.

Nate nodded, his brain cataloging every detail, every nuance. There was work to be done, and the Everharts were just getting started.

The dusty glow of the stage lights cast long, angular shadows across the wooden floorboards as Nate leaned against a mock brick wall, his eyes scanning the room. The rehearsal had ended, but the theatre hummed with an undercurrent of tension and whispered secrets. Amy was huddled with Susan and Cynthia, their heads bent close together in fervent discussion. He could feel it, the invisible threads of camaraderie weaving tighter around them, drawing them into the fold.

"Think we're getting somewhere?" Martin's voice broke through Nate's contemplation, his figure emerging from the dim backstage area, script in hand.

"Depends on what you mean by 'somewhere,'" Nate replied, pushing off from the wall. The smell of sawdust and paint thickened the air, a tangible reminder of the facade they were all part of.

"Information is trickling in," he continued, watching Robert fiddle with a prop in the corner, the man's movements hesitant and jerky. "But we're still dancing on the surface."

"Surface is better than nothin'," Martin quipped, but his smile didn't quite reach his eyes. He glanced toward Amy and the others before lowering his voice. "Some folks here... they're scared, Nate. More than just superstitious jitters, ya know?"

Nate folded his arms, nodding slowly. "Fear can be a powerful motivator." His mind raced, piecing together the puzzle; every fragment of overheard dialogue, each subtle shift in demeanor, a potential clue.

"Or a weapon," Martin added, his gaze drifting to the darkened auditorium seats, a sea of emptiness that seemed to watch them with quiet anticipation.

"Both," Nate said, his tone even, but inside, his thoughts churned like a storm. Fear was the lock, and trust, the key. And they were inching closer to fitting it into place.

"Goodnight, Nate." Martin slapped him on the shoulder, a brotherly gesture that belied the unease lurking beneath.

"Night, Martin." Nate watched him go, the sound of his footsteps fading into silence.

Amy approached then, her face alight with a mixture of excitement and determination. "Susan's opening up. She mentioned some financial irregularities, hinted at more."

"Good," Nate replied, his heart rate ticking up a notch. "We tread carefully. One wrong step and..."

"Everything unravels." Amy finished his sentence, her green eyes reflecting the stage lights like twin emeralds.

He reached out, brushing a strand of red hair back from her face. Their mission was clear, their resolve unshaken. But the path ahead was shadowed with risks they couldn't fully anticipate.

"Let's call it a night," Nate suggested, his voice low. "We regroup, come back fresh."

"Agreed." She took his hand, their fingers intertwining naturally.

As they made their way through the maze of set pieces, the whisper of curtains and creaking floorboards accompanied them, a silent audience to their departure. The door closed behind them with a soft click, sealing the theatre and its secrets in the darkness once more.

Outside, the night air was brisk, the moon a thin crescent above. They walked side by side down the deserted street, the echo of their footsteps a steady rhythm in the quiet.

"Tomorrow, we dig deeper," Amy said, her breath a white vapor in the chill.

"Until we strike the truth," Nate affirmed, squeezing her hand.

And with that, they stepped into the night, the promise of unseen challenges veiling the road ahead, the thrill of the hunt fueling their every step.

Chapter 4

Nate and Amy slipped through the heavy velvet curtains of the Theater, their eyes sweeping across the bustling rehearsal space. A cacophony of lines being recited, stage directions called out, and the occasional clatter of a prop falling to the ground filled the air. They moved with purpose yet unobtrusive, like shadows mingling with the light.

"Keep your eyes peeled," Nate murmured, the corners of his mouth twitching in the faintest smile. His gaze darted from face to face, analyzing, assessing. He knew the devil was in the details; the way a hand fluttered nervously, a gaze that lingered too long, a laugh too sharp.

"Always do," Amy replied, her voice low and steady. Her red hair, pulled back in a practical ponytail, did little to dim the vibrant energy she exuded. She scanned the room with practiced ease, the jigsaw pieces of the puzzle before them begging to be assembled.

The pair wove through clusters of actors rehearsing lines, sidestepping a prop table laden with an assortment of items—a fake dagger here, a vintage telephone there. With every step, they took in the dynamics of the group, the ebb and flow of relationships playing out in front of them.

"Excuse me," came a gentle voice tinged with the warmth of years spent nurturing. "You must be new."

They turned to see Diane Peterson standing before them, a welcoming smile on her face that crinkled the corners of her kind blue eyes. Her short, curly blonde hair framed her face, softening her expression even further.

"Hi, I'm Nate," he said, extending a hand, which she took in a firm, motherly grip. "And this is Amy."

"Delighted to meet you both," Diane said, releasing his hand to offer the same kindness to Amy. "I'm Diane, I like to think of myself as the den mother around here."

"We appreciate the welcome," Amy said, her voice threaded with the sincerity of someone who knew the value of trust. "It's our first time in a place like this."

Diane nodded, her eyes hinting at the layers of caution built from past hardships. "Well, we're a family here. Look out for one another." Her gaze lingered on them a moment longer, searching, perhaps, for a glimpse of the stories they carried.

"Thank you, Diane," Nate said, his tone appreciative yet measured. "We're glad to be part of it."

As Diane was called away by a sudden commotion near the stage, Nate and Amy exchanged a quick, knowing glance. The con was in motion, and the threads of deceit they sought to unravel had just found two new weavers adept at crafting their own tapestry of truth within the lies.

Amy's gaze drifted across the room, snagging on a fervent exchange by the far wall. Martin Brown was in his element, arms gesturing wildly as he delved into the psyche of his latest character. His voice, a blend of passion and precision, cut through the ambient noise of the theater.

"Every action, every line—it's all driven by Jasper's loss," Martin declared, eyes ablaze. The cast member opposite him nodded, absorbed.

"Like he's chasing ghosts," Amy murmured, more to herself than to Nate.

"Or being chased by them," Nate added quietly, his mind already weaving this new thread into their investigation.

Before they could dissect Martin's performance further, a burst of laughter bubbled up nearby. Cynthia Davis bounced towards them, her smile as wide as the stage itself.

"Hey! I'm Cynthia!" she chirped, thrusting out a hand adorned with glittery nail polish. "New faces are always a treat!"

"Nice to meet you, Cynthia," Nate replied, taking her hand with a grin that matched her enthusiasm. "I'm Nate, and this is Amy."

"Thrilled to have you both here!" Cynthia beamed. Her blue eyes sparkled with an innocence that seemed almost out of place amidst the backdrop of potential deceit.

"Seems like quite the production," Amy said, pivoting smoothly into the role of the curious newcomer.

"Best family I've ever had," Cynthia gushed. "You're gonna love it!"

Nate exchanged a look with Amy. Family was a word they'd heard before—a masquerade for hidden agendas. But there was no time to ponder; the rehearsal was moving forward, and so must they.

Susan Thompson's voice sliced through the hum of backstage chatter. "Places, people! We're on a tight schedule." She clapped her hands with military precision—a sharp staccato that commanded attention.

Nate watched as the cast scrambled into position, their movements infused with a mixture of fear and respect. Susan stalked between the rows of seats, her gaze scrutinizing every detail, from the placement of props to the posture of actors. Her sharp green eyes missed nothing, a predator amongst thespians.

"Remember, your cues are gospel," she barked, notepad in hand, the pen tapping an insistent rhythm against the paper.

"Efficiency incarnate," Amy muttered, impressed despite herself.

"Or tyranny," Nate countered, his eyes narrowing as he observed Susan's interactions, searching for cracks in her armor.

Before he could delve deeper, a burst of color swept into their periphery. Robert Johnson, flamboyantly dressed, approached them with a bounce in his step. "You must be the new additions," he said, extending a hand adorned with rings that caught the stage lights.

"Guilty as charged," Nate replied, shaking Robert's hand firmly.

"Robert Johnson, costume designer extraordinaire," he introduced himself with a flourish. "And you are?"

"Nate and Amy," Amy supplied, her smile genuine.

"Delighted!" Robert exclaimed. He launched into a tirade about his latest creation. "A veritable nightmare, this one. Historical accuracy meets modern flair. Try telling that to a director who thinks polyester is period-appropriate!"

"Sounds challenging," Amy sympathized, her eyes taking in the sketches Robert pulled from his portfolio. The lines were impeccable, the vision bold.

"Challenging, yes, but thrilling!" Robert's eyes sparkled with passion. "To give life to characters through fabric and thread—there's nothing like it."

"Except when the fabric fights back," Nate quipped, earning a hearty laugh from Robert.

"Ah, you understand!" Robert clapped Nate on the shoulder, camaraderie quick to bloom. "Now, if only the budget would stop fighting me."

"Common enemy?" Amy asked, her tone light but her mind cataloging Robert's grievances.

"Alas, the most formidable," Robert sighed dramatically. "But we persevere!"

"Indeed, we do," Nate agreed, his gaze shifting back to Susan. He noted her preoccupation with control, how it might be leveraged. The rehearsal space was rife with dynamics and tensions, a puzzle begging to be solved.

"Keep your friends close," Amy whispered to him, nodding subtly at Robert, who was now animatedly describing the texture of a particularly rebellious velvet.

"And your costume designers closer," Nate finished, a plan beginning to take shape in his analytical mind.

The rehearsal space buzzed with activity, a hive of artists in motion. A sudden hush swept over the room, like an invisible wave pressing down on the chatter and laughter. Nate's eyes flicked to the entrance, senses sharpening. She arrived.

Sapphire. The drag queen was a vision, her elegantly coiffed hair framing a face painted to exaggerated, flawless perfection. Her gown, a cascade of sequins and feathers, shimmered with each calculated step. Eyes followed her, as if drawn by strings she held with effortless grace.

"Darlings," Sapphire's voice cut through the quiet, rich and velvety. "Apologies for my fashionably late entrance."

"Typical Sapphire," a stagehand muttered, rolling his eyes. But even the complaint rang with a tone of admiration.

Amy leaned closer to Nate, her whisper barely audible. "Watch her," she said.

Nate nodded, his gaze never leaving the figure at the room's center. Sapphire exchanged air kisses with Diane, who beamed under the attention. A laugh here, a touch there, each gesture deliberate. To the untrained eye, Sapphire mingled with ease. But Nate saw more. Saw how Sapphire's fingers lingered on Martin's shoulder, a silent communicator of power. Saw the way her eyes narrowed slightly when Cynthia approached, calculating the threat of youthful ambition.

"See that?" Amy's voice was low, her skills as an investigative journalist kicking in.

"Every move has a purpose," Nate murmured in response.

A brief exchange with Susan followed, their heads close together. Terms and conditions were being set, not in words but in nods. Sapphire then turned to Robert, her smile wide. Yet, the costume designer's enthusiasm dimmed ever so slightly under her gaze.

"Charm as a weapon," Amy noted, her eyes darting between the interactions.

"Or a distraction," Nate countered.

They watched as Sapphire sauntered through the group, leaving whispers and glances in her wake. Every action was a thread pulled tight, every word a knot tied with precision. The drag queen's presence loomed large, her shadow touching each person differently.

"Agendas hidden beneath silk and rouge," Nate observed with a hint of respect.

"Let's not get caught in her web," Amy replied.

Together, they studied the enigmatic figure, minds racing to untangle the web of manipulation before it ensnared them too. Sapphire, the captivating enigma, played her part with flair, unaware that two more players had entered the stage.

Nate mingled, a glass of water in hand, nodding along to the hum of rehearsal chaos. Amy stood a few feet away, her laugh genuine as she shared an anecdote with Cynthia. They were moths fluttering near the flame, seeking warmth without getting scorched.

"Stagecraft seems like your second skin," Nate said to Robert, who was adjusting a mannequin's extravagant costume nearby.

"Every stitch tells a story," Robert replied, his fingers dancing on the fabric. "Takes a keen eye to see it."

Nate watched, storing every detail. Robert spoke of challenges—budget cuts, last-minute changes. His words painted a broader picture, one filled with stress lines and late nights.

"Art is sacrifice," Robert concluded, his smile tight.

"Sometimes more than it should be," Nate agreed, his tone light but eyes sharp.

Amy drifted back to Nate's side, seamlessly taking over the conversation. Her knack for inquiry disguised as casual interest.

"Such dedication," she observed, her gaze sweeping the room, landing on Susan. The stage manager was a force, her voice cutting through the air, shaping order from chaos.

"Without her, we'd be lost," Robert admitted, glancing at Susan with something akin to reverence.

"Or free?" Nate quipped, drawing a short-lived smirk from the costume designer.

Across the room, Diane gathered a small flock under her wing, her stories flowing like honey. Nate and Amy approached, the group parting to welcome them.

"Back in my day, we made do with what we had," Diane reminisced, her blue eyes alight with memories. "We were family, bound by love for the craft."

"Seems you've kept that spirit alive here," Amy remarked, her voice warm.

"Couldn't have survived otherwise," Diane responded, her curls bouncing as she nodded emphatically. "This place, these people—they're my heart."

"Cherished connections," Nate mused, scanning the faces around Diane. Bonds, strong yet fragile, ripe for exploitation.

"Indeed," Diane confirmed with a soft smile, oblivious to the undercurrents Nate sensed.

Her anecdotes wove a tapestry of years spent in the theater—a haven for some, a battleground for others. Diane's gratitude shone through, her tales punctuated by laughter and the occasional sigh. It was clear: this community was her world.

"Must be tough, safeguarding such a legacy," Amy said, her journalistic instincts probing gently.

"Keeps me young," Diane chuckled, brushing off the depth of her responsibility. "And besides, we look out for each other here."

Nate exchanged a glance with Amy. In their line of work, "looking out" often meant look

Amy leaned against a backstage pillar, her gaze sweeping across the rehearsal hall like a hawk scouting prey. Martin's voice cut through the ambient noise, crisp and commanding as he argued a point about his character's inner turmoil. Her eyes fixed on him; she had to admit, his passion was magnetic.

"Hey, you," Martin said, suddenly beside her. His presence was a jolt to her senses—too close, too intense.

"Martin." She kept her voice even, betraying none of the surprise that fluttered in her chest.

"Care for a coffee break?" He gestured toward the side exit, a playful challenge in his dark eyes.

"Lead the way." Amy fell into step beside him, their strides matching. The hallway outside the rehearsal space was cooler, quieter, a respite from the constant motion within.

"Black with two sugars, right?" Martin asked, recalling their earlier conversation. Amy raised an eyebrow, impressed despite herself.

"Good memory."

"Actors," he said with a shrug. "We remember our lines—and our co-stars' preferences."

Their banter was easy, a game of verbal tennis. But Amy's mind was working, angles and edges sharp as she probed for openings, for clues.

"Must be thrilling, being the lead," she ventured, sipping the steaming coffee he handed her.

"Thrilling and terrifying," Martin admitted, leaning against the counter. "The pressure is immense, but I live for it."

"Live dangerously, then?"

"Always." His smile was quicksilver, and for a moment, Amy allowed herself to enjoy it—before snapping back to the task at hand.

"Speaking of living dangerously," Cynthia bubbled up beside them, her blonde hair a halo in the dim lighting. She clutched a well-worn script to her chest, blue eyes wide with dreams too big for the small theater.

"Is this your first production, Cynthia?" Amy asked, slipping into the role of curious newcomer.

"Second, actually!" Cynthia's enthusiasm spilled over. "But this time feels different. Like the start of something big. You know?"

"Big dreams often start in small places," Amy encouraged, her red locks catching the light as she nodded.

"Exactly!" Cynthia beamed. "One day I'll see my name in lights, Amy. I just know it."

"Keep that fire burning," Martin added, his tone supportive but edged with a reality check. "The path to fame can be treacherous."

"Thanks! I will." Oblivious to the veiled warning, Cynthia bounced away, her energy infectious but tinged with innocence—a target painted on her back.

Amy's grip tightened around her coffee cup. Beneath the laughter and camaraderie, shadows lurked, waiting to pounce on the unwary. And Cynthia, bright and trusting, might as well have been walking blindfolded through a minefield.

"Back to the grind?" Martin asked, breaking into her thoughts.

"Let's do it." Amy set down her empty cup, her resolve steeling. There would be no casualties on her watch—not if she could help it. She followed him back inside, ready to peel back the curtain on the darker acts playing out behind the scenes.

Nate leaned against a cold, brick wall, his eyes tracking Susan Thompson as she moved across the stage with the precision of a chess grandmaster. Her hands were swift, sorting through an array of props, her green eyes scanning each item before meticulously placing it in its designated spot. He appreciated that kind of dedication—it was something he recognized, a mirror to his own relentless drive.

"Everything has to be perfect," Susan muttered to herself, unaware of Nate's watchful gaze. She checked her clipboard again, her brow furrowing as she noted something that only she could see was out of place. Adjusting a prop on the table, she nodded, satisfied at last.

"Details," Nate whispered under his breath. "She lives for them."

His focus was broken by a soft tap on his shoulder. He turned to find Robert Johnson standing there, his dark hair perfectly coiffed and a sly smile playing on his lips.

"Quite the watchdog, aren't you?" Robert teased, his voice low but carrying an undertone of camaraderie.

"Observant," Nate corrected with a nonchalant shrug, not giving away his true purpose.

"Speaking of observant," Robert began, leaning in closer, "have you heard about the latest hiccup with our production?" His enthusiasm for sharing was palpable, the gossip almost spilling out of him like water from a breached dam.

"Can't say that I have," Nate replied, his interest piqued, sensing an opportunity to glean some valuable intel.

"Word is we've got issues with our set designer—creative differences," Robert confided, air-quoting the last two words. "Thinks the theme's too dark for the usual crowd. Wants more... sparkle."

"Sparkle doesn't sound like a bad thing," Nate said casually, probing for more without seeming eager.

"Maybe not, but it's causing delays. And between you and me," Robert glanced around before continuing, "this show's budget? It's ballooning faster than you can say 'overrun.'"

Nate's mind raced. Budget overruns could point to financial trouble, or worse, someone skimming off the top. It was a thread worth pulling.

"Challenges like that can make or break a production," Nate mused aloud, offering just enough to keep Robert talking.

"Break, more likely," Robert sighed dramatically, though Nate detected real concern beneath the theatrics. "If we don't sort it out soon, this whole house of cards might just collapse."

"Let's hope it doesn't come to that," Nate replied, filing away every scrap of information. The pieces were starting to fall into place, and with each new detail, the bigger picture grew clearer. Someone was playing a dangerous game behind the curtain, and Nate was determined to expose it—before anyone else got hurt.

Sapphire glided onto the stage, the spotlight caressing her sequined dress into a million dancing reflections. She paused—a breath, a heartbeat—then the music swelled. Her voice, rich and potent, wove through the air, an audible spell binding the room.

Nate leaned against the back wall, arms folded, his gaze fixed on the captivating performer. Amy stood beside him, her sharp eyes not missing a beat, a slight tilt to her head betraying her intrigue. They had seen countless acts, but Sapphire, she was different. This wasn't just another performance; it was a statement, a display of power.

Around them, the theater group was entranced, hanging on every note, every fluid movement. Sapphire commanded the stage as if born there, yet beneath the glamour, Nate sensed layers. Layers that spoke of secrets and hidden agendas. What was she after? Control, influence, or something more?

Amy nudged him, a silent signal. Her eyes darted from Sapphire to the captivated faces in the crowd, then back again. She was thinking it too. There was more to this performance than met the eye. It was a show within a show, and they were here to uncover the unseen act.

The song reached its crescendo, Sapphire's presence filling the space with such intensity it almost felt tangible. When the final note hung in the air, the silence before applause felt like the whole world holding its breath. Then, thunderous claps erupted, breaking the spell.

"Bravo!" someone shouted, and the sentiment rippled through the group.

As the adoration washed over Sapphire, Nate caught a flicker of something in her eyes. Triumph? Satisfaction? It was gone before he could decipher it. He exchanged a look with Amy. They needed to dig deeper, peel back the veneer of this too-perfect scene.

Sapphire took a bow, the light playing off her gown, casting a glow that seemed to reach every corner of the darkened theater. Then, with a smile that promised both allure and mystery, she sauntered offstage, leaving a trail of questions in her wake.

Nate straightened up. Time to get to work. Sapphire held keys to doors they hadn't even found yet, and Nate and Amy were going to turn every lock.

Chapter 5

Nate leaned against the kitchen counter, tapping a rhythm on the laminate with his fingers—a telltale sign of bubbling excitement. Amy watched him, her own heart racing with a mix of adrenaline and anticipation.

"Remember, these theater folks, they live for passion, breathe drama," Nate said, his eyes sparkling with that charismatic glint that had swayed tougher crowds than an amateur acting troupe.

"Passion, got it," Amy replied, tucking a strand of fiery red hair behind her ear. "We'll give them the performance of a lifetime."

"Right," he affirmed, straightening up. "We don't just want those roles; we need to become Bob and Suzie. Bond with the cast. Find their weak spots."

Amy nodded. She thought back to her investigative days, how each detail could make or break a story. Here, the details would build their characters.

"Bob's your average Joe, but with a twist," Nate continued, already slipping into the persona with ease. "And Suzie—she's resilient yet vulnerable. It's a fine line."

"Which I'll walk like a tightrope," Amy interjected, her voice tinged with the steel of conviction.

"Then let's get to the stage," Nate said, offering his hand. Together, they left their safe haven, stepping out into the deception they were about to weave.

***

The theater loomed before them, its old brick facade a testament to countless stories told within its walls. They joined the throng of hopefuls, each one murmuring lines or stretching limbs, lost in personal rituals.

Nate felt the energy, palpable as electricity in the air. He glanced at Amy, her posture poised, ready to take on the world—or at least this small part of it. This was their arena now; time to play their parts.

"Let's mingle, find our marks," Nate whispered. They split up, Nate shaking hands, flashing his most genuine smile, while Amy chatted with a group of actors, laughter pealing from her lips like she'd known them for years.

They were no longer Nathaniel and Amelia Everhart; they were prospective members of this ensemble, each interaction calculated to endear, to ingratiate, to camouflage.

As other names were called, tension strung tighter through the room. Each audition was another step closer to theirs. With every passing minute, Nate and Amy wove themselves further into the fabric of this theatrical tapestry, threads indistinguishable from the original.

"Everhart, Nathaniel," a voice eventually rang out. "Everhart, Amelia."

The moment of truth. Nate took a deep breath, exchanged a look with Amy that held the weight of their mission, and stepped forward into the limelight.

Nate strode onto the stage, his gait confident, every step measured—a predator in the guise of prey. Amy followed, her movements a dance between shadows and light, a whisper of silk against the backdrop of anticipation. The director's gaze, sharp as a hawk's, tracked their approach, skepticism etched deep within his furrowed brow.

"Begin," he commanded, terse and unyielding.

The words of Bob and Suzie leapt to life, Nate's voice a chameleon, adapting, shifting with ease from one emotion to the next. He was no longer Nathaniel Everhart; he was Bob—a man of simple desires entangled in a web far beyond his ken. Amy breathed Suzie into existence, her eyes pools of vulnerability rimmed with steel. Together, they painted a picture of trust and treachery, innocence used as fodder in a game played by giants.

The air crackled with the force of their delivery, each line a thread spun into a tapestry of deceit and devotion. They were not just actors; they were alchemists, transmuting words into raw, palpable feeling. The director leaned forward, the stern lines of his face softening, ensnared by the gravity of their performance.

"Scene," Nate declared, the word reverberating like a shot in the silence that followed.

A beat passed, then two, before applause erupted, tentative at first, then swelling into genuine appreciation. Group members exchanged looks of approval, their earlier curiosity blooming into respect. These newcomers had done more than perform—they had transformed the mundane into magic, leaving an indelible mark upon their audience.

"Thank you, Nate, Amy," the director said, standing now, the timbre of his voice betraying a hint of surprise. "That was...compelling. You've brought something unique to these roles."

He extended his hand, and they shook it, their grips firm—pledges of commitment to a cause yet unseen. "We'll be in touch," he assured them, a promise hanging between them like a bridge over chasms of uncertainty.

"Thank you for the opportunity," Amy replied, her tone earnest, eyes gleaming with the thrill of the hunt.

As they exited, the weight of the director's gaze lingered, heavy with thoughts unspoken. They had taken the first step into a world veiled in velvet curtains and whispered secrets—a world where they would unravel the threads of Sapphire's grand design.

Stepping out of the audition room, the echoes of their performance still danced in the air behind them. Nate's eyes scanned the hallway, a strategic sweep taking in every detail—the nervous tics of waiting performers, the hushed conversations, the furtive glances that followed them. Amy's posture was poised, a sleek predator who had just shared a glimpse of her claws and now walked away, masking satisfaction with practiced nonchalance.

They navigated through the corridors of ambition, their strides synchronized—a duet of purpose. Nate could feel the energy buzzing from Amy, a silent signal of success pulsating between them. They had planted the seeds of trust; roots were already spreading unseen beneath the surface.

The heavy door to the theater creaked open, and they stepped out into the cool embrace of evening air, leaving behind the glow of stage lights and the scent of anticipation. On the bustling street, they were just two more faces in the crowd again, but beneath the mundane façade, a current of excitement surged.

A stolen glance exchanged, loaded with unspoken words. Nate's eyes met Amy's—steel sharpening steel. It was a momentary link, locking in the resolve that coursed through their veins. They knew the game they were playing was fraught with risk, each move on the chessboard critical, each piece a pawn in their hands.

In the fading light, as the city's pulse beat around them, their own hearts matched the rhythm, steady and sure. The challenge loomed ahead, its shadow stretching long across their path. But together, they stood ready to chase the truth through a maze of lies, to peel back layers of deception.

Tonight, the act was done. Tomorrow, the real performance would begin.

***

The city's neon lights blurred past as Nate navigated the streets, his mind rifling through the day's heist of emotions. Amy rode shotgun, her gaze fixed on the rearview mirror's reflection—a hunter scouting for tails. None followed. Their charade at the theater had been airtight.

"Tonight was just the overture," Nate said, breaking the silence that cocooned them since they left the audition room.

"Agreed," Amy replied, her voice steady, "but we've got our foot in the door. Now we need to wedge it open."

Nate nodded, the weight of their task pressing against his thoughts. The theater group was their way in, a nest where Sapphire harbored secrets. To pluck those secrets, they'd have to blend into the fabric of the troupe, become threads in Sapphire's twisted tapestry.

"Once we're in, we'll need to be careful," Amy continued. "Sapphire is no fool. She—"

"He," Nate corrected out of habit, thinking of Stanley Richards behind the queen's mask.

"Right, he's cunning." Amy turned to him, her eyes narrowing. "We need to think two steps ahead, anticipate the moves."

The car pulled into the garage, its headlights slicing through the darkness before flicking off. They sat in the stillness, the engine ticking as it cooled. This was more than a con; it was personal, a quest rooted in past injustices that fueled their present resolve.

Home now became base camp, a place to hone their strategy. The living room transformed into a war room, with notes scattered across the coffee table and laptops aglow with blueprints and background checks.

"Bob and Suzie," Nate mused aloud, referring to their audition personas. "Simple parts, but they'll give us access."

"Exactly," Amy agreed, tapping away at her keyboard. "Through them, we observe, we listen. We gather every scrap we can without raising suspicion."

"Then we use what we find to unravel Sapphire's web," Nate concluded, his fingers drumming against the tabletop.

They worked into the night, mapping out their next moves, plotting how to ingratiate themselves further into the group. With each click of the keyboard, with each stroke of the pen, they wove themselves deeper into the narrative.

Their successful audition was the key that unlocked the door. Now, stepping through it, they were poised to dive into the heart of the theater group. There, in the midst of lines and rehearsals, they would search for the truth hidden within the performances, within the camaraderie, within Sapphire's gleaming façade.

This was their mission: infiltrate, investigate, expose. Every act from here on out had to be flawless. The stakes were high, but so was their determination. They wouldn't rest until the curtain fell on Sapphire's final show.

***

Nate clicked the laptop shut, the sharp snap echoing in the silence. He leaned back, rubbing his temples where the tension had knotted. Amy glanced over, a silent question in her gaze, her own laptop casting a pale glow on her determined features.

"Got enough to start with?" she asked, her voice low but threaded with excitement.

"More than enough." Nate's reply was terse, a smile tugging at his lips despite the fatigue. "Sapphire won't even see us coming."

They rose, stretching limbs cramped from hours of strategizing. The room hummed with the electric charge of their intent, papers and digital trails weaving a web of their making. In the shadows, they were two silhouettes bristling with potential, ready to spring into action.

"Tomorrow, we blend in," said Amy, her eyes gleaming like coals. "We become Bob and Suzie. We earn their trust."

"Then we strike at the heart," Nate added, his jaw set. They knew the roles they played now were crucial, each move calculated and every word measured. This wasn't just another con; it was a mission, a lifeline to those ensnared by Sapphire's deceit.

Their hands touched, fingers intertwining in a pact of shared purpose. They were partners, in crime and in justice, their bond the unspoken strength beneath their resolve.

"Time to bring down the house," Nate whispered, the words a promise in the darkness.

Amy nodded, her smile fierce. "And save the innocents caught in the crossfire."

They turned off the lights, the room plunging into darkness, save for the streetlight streaming through the window. It cast long shadows that danced across the floor, mirroring the anticipation that thrummed through their veins.

Out into the night they moved, the chapter closing behind them with an air of expectancy. The stage was set, the players in position, and as Nate and Amy stepped out, the city's heartbeat seemed to pulse with their own. Tomorrow, they would act. Tomorrow, they would unravel the truth.

And nothing could stop them now.

Chapter 6

Nate and Amy strode into the rehearsal space, a hive of creative chaos. The cacophony of lines being rehearsed echoed off the walls. The scent of sawdust and paint lingered in the air from set construction. They exchanged a glance, their shared purpose unspoken but understood.

"Showtime," Nate murmured under his breath, a half-smile flickering across his face.

Amy nodded, her eyes scanning the room with practiced precision. They weaved through clusters of actors, dodging a prop table laden with old telephones and feather boas. Their steps were purposeful, their presence commanding yet unobtrusive.

They spotted Diane Peterson near the back of the room, her hands animated as she guided a pair of young actors through a complex scene. Her blonde curls bounced with every emphatic gesture, her blue eyes reflecting the fervor of her passion for the craft.

"Ms. Peterson?" Nate called out, his voice cutting through the din with ease.

Diane turned, her expression shifting from focus to warm recognition. "Nate, Amy! What a pleasure to see you both again."

"We wouldn't miss it for the world," Amy replied, her tone genuine. She admired Diane's commitment, the kind that could only be forged through years of perseverance.

"Your dedication is remarkable," Nate said, leaning in slightly, "It must take incredible resilience to keep a group like this together."

Diane chuckled, a hint of weariness in her laugh. "Well, when you love something deeply, you fight for it. You understand how that is, don't you?"

"More than you know," Nate agreed, his eyes locking onto hers. He sensed the layers beneath her sunny disposition, the caution born from past trials.

"Tell us about your journey in theater," Amy encouraged, her voice laced with intrigue. "Every production has its story, right?"

"Indeed, it does," Diane sighed, a distant look crossing her features as if she were about to recount tales of countless battlefields. "But let's walk while we talk. Duty calls, and the curtain waits for no one."

As they strolled alongside Diane, Nate and Amy listened intently. Every word, every inflection was a potential clue, a piece of the puzzle they were determined to solve.

Amy spotted Cynthia Davis perched on the edge of the stage, script in hand. Her eyes were alight with a dreamer's glow, her blonde hair cascading around her shoulders like spun gold. Amy approached, the clack of her heels muted by the soft hum of backstage machinery.

"Mind if I join you?" Amy asked, flashing a smile as genuine as the one she reserved for Nate after a successful day.

"Of course!" Cynthia beamed, shifting to make room. "Actually, I could use some company."

They fell into conversation easily, words ebbing and flowing like a well-rehearsed duet. Cynthia spoke of her passion for acting, her voice bubbling with excitement. Amy nodded, interjecting with questions that coaxed out dreams tinged with naivety.

"Acting is my call," Cynthia declared, clutching the script to her chest. "I want to touch people's hearts, you know?"

"I do," Amy said, her gaze steady. She saw the open book of Cynthia's ambition and feared the pages might be torn out by exploitation's cruel hand. "Keep that fire burning. It'll light your way to the stars."

Across the room, Nate leaned against a prop table, his attention on Martin Brown, who was animatedly discussing his latest role. Martin's gestures were grand, his voice resonating with the depth of a man who lived for the spotlight.

"Leading a cast must feel like steering a ship through a storm," Nate posited, keeping his tone light yet probing.

"It's exhilarating," Martin admitted, his dark eyes sparking with fervor. "You ride the highs and lows, but standing ovations? They make it all worth it."

"Must take a toll, though," Nate ventured, watching for any flicker of discord or strain.

"Sometimes," Martin conceded with a shrug of his broad shoulders. "But when the audience is with you, it's magic."

Nate nodded, his mind cataloging every nuance. The camaraderie masked vulnerabilities, the shine that could dull under pressure. He stowed the insights away, ammunition for later.

"Keep conjuring that magic, Martin," Nate encouraged, a conspiratorial grin on his face. "The world needs more of it."

"I will," Martin replied, clapping Nate on the shoulder before returning to his rehearsal, a king retaking his throne.

Nate's grin faded as he retreated into the shadows. In the wings of the theater, secrets whispered and motives hid. He and Amy would shine a light, expose the deceit festering beneath the surface. Together, they'd ensure this production's final act revealed truth over tragedy.

Amy's eyes swept over the set, sketches of grandeur marred by the realities of frayed edges and worn props. The stage manager, Susan Thompson, stood amidst the organized chaos, her sharp green eyes flicking from the clipboard in her hands to the actors rehearsing their lines.

"Need a hand?" Amy asked, stepping forward, her own gaze as meticulous as a hawk's.

Susan glanced up, a crease of concern softening as she appraised Amy's genuine offer. "If you're willing," she replied, the weight of countless tasks momentarily lifting.

"Where do you need me?" Amy rolled up her sleeves, her posture all business, every inch the investigative journalist she once was, now channeling her skills into the nuances of stagecraft.

"Props table," Susan pointed, relief etched in her voice. "Checklist is on the clipboard."

"Got it." Amy's fingers danced over the items with precision, ticking off boxes, straightening misplaced trinkets, her attention snagging on inconsistencies like a detective sifting for clues.

In another corner of the theater, Nate leaned against the wall, his attention focused on Robert Johnson, whose fingers fluttered over fabric swatches with the flair of a maestro commanding an orchestra. The costume designer's pompadour bobbed as he animatedly described his vision for the production's wardrobe.

"Artistry in every stitch," Nate remarked, his voice tinged with respect. He understood the power of details; in costumes, as in crimes, they were telling.

"Thanks," Robert beamed, pride swelling in his chest. "I try to weave a bit of each character's essence into their attire. It helps the actors inhabit their roles, you know?"

"Smart," Nate nodded, his dark eyes absorbing Robert's enthusiasm, his mind noting the intimate connection between garment and wearer—a link that could bind or betray.

"Costume design's a subtle craft," Robert continued, oblivious to Nate's probing undercurrent. "It's about enhancing the story, not stealing the scene."

"Unless the scene calls for it," Nate quipped, watching Robert's reaction closely.

"Exactly!" Robert laughed, delighted by Nate's understanding. "You get it."

Nate smiled, his charismatic presence easily engaging Robert's trust, while inwardly he remained vigilant, scanning for any thread that might unravel the mystery enshrouding the theater group.

Nate strode onto the stage, script in hand, squinting beneath the stark lights. Lines flowed from him like water from a burst pipe, slick and unstoppable. Amy mirrored his intensity from her position downstage, eyes locked on her counterpart, every movement purposeful, calculated.

"Bravo!" Diane's voice pierced the rehearsal hall as the scene came to a close. Murmurs of approval rippled through the cast. Nate and Amy exchanged a quick glance, satisfaction mingling with the adrenaline of performance. Their cover was holding — more than holding, it was convincing.

"Natural talents," Martin Brown murmured, eyeing them with a mix of appreciation and something else — an edge of competitiveness that Nate filed away for later consideration.

"Thanks, Martin." Nate replied.

Amy's laughter danced from the wings, light but not without substance. "All the world's a stage," she quipped, winking at Cynthia Davis, who stood nearby, script clutched to her chest.

"Seems we're all playing our parts well," Cynthia responded, the subtext of her words not lost on Amy.

The break bell tolled, and the group scattered like leaves in the wind. Nate snagged a sandwich, Amy by his side, their bodies angled toward the cluster of actors congregating around the snack table. Casual, almost too casual, they leaned in.

"Quite the series of mishaps lately, huh?" Amy ventured, her tone light but probing as she unwrapped her lunch.

Diane pursed her lips, eyes darting to a spot over Amy's shoulder before settling back. "Yes, it's been... unsettling."

"Any theories?" Nate asked, pausing mid-bite, his gaze steady.

"Bad luck," Martin offered, shrugging, his nonchalance failing to mask the tightness in his jaw.

"Or bad blood," Susan chimed in from behind her clipboard, not looking up.

"Bad blood?" Amy echoed, head tilting, her red hair catching the fluorescent lighting.

"Metaphorically speaking," Susan clarified, but her eyes flickered with something unreadable.

"Of course," Nate said, filing away the slip. He took another bite, chewing thoughtfully.

"Costumes going missing, lights malfunctioning..." Robert trailed off, counting off on his fingers. His concern seemed genuine, but Nate noticed the way his eyes didn't quite meet theirs.

"Accidents can happen," Nate mused aloud, watching the reactions play across their faces like a silent movie.

"Indeed," Sapphire interjected, her voice carrying an edge as she swept past, her attention momentarily caught by an open Facebook page over a fellow actor's shoulder. Nate's eyes narrowed imperceptibly.

"Anyway, let's hope for smoother sailing from here on out," Amy said, raising her sandwich in a mock toast.

"Here's to that," Diane replied, her smile tight as she sipped her water.

As the group dispersed, Nate chewed over more than just his lunch. Each interaction, each reaction was a piece of the puzzle. The game was afoot, and he and Amy were already several moves ahead.

Nate slung an arm around Amy as they strolled into the cozy living room of Diane's apartment, where the post-rehearsal gathering buzzed with a warm, inviting energy. The scent of fresh coffee mingled with laughter and the faint hint of stage makeup that clung to the air. Bottles of wine stood at attention on the counter, glasses clinking in a symphony of camaraderie.

"Great job today, everyone," Nate proclaimed, the group's approving nods feeding the room's growing sense of unity. "This production's going to be stellar."

"Thanks to our newest members," Martin said, raising his glass toward Nate and Amy. His muscles relaxed from the day's performance, but his eyes still held the spark of the spotlight.

Amy leaned against the kitchen island, her gaze sweeping over the faces illuminated by the soft glow of under-cabinet lighting. "It's always a rush, stepping into someone else's shoes," she mused, sharing a knowing look with Cynthia, who nodded eagerly.

"Exactly!" Cynthia beamed, her enthusiasm contagious. "Every role is a chance to live another life."

"Or uncover one," Susan added, her smirk playful yet edged with the precision of her stage management skills. Her green eyes flickered knowingly at Amy, a silent acknowledgment of the shared hunt for truth beneath the surface.

"Speaking of lives," Robert chimed in, refilling his glass, "what stories brought you two to our little troupe?"

Nate exchanged a glance with Amy, his dark eyes glinting with the thrill of weaving their fabricated pasts into the tapestry of their mission. "Military brat turned tech wizard," he began, the corners of his lips tilting up in a half-smile.

"Wow," murmured Diane, her admiration apparent even as her seasoned skepticism lingered like a shadow. "That's quite the journey."

"Mine's less code and more headlines," Amy continued, her voice carrying the cadence of someone who'd seen the darker corners of the world. "Investigative journalism is in my blood—started after my dad was caught in a web of lies."

"Nothing like fighting for the underdog," Martin said, nodding solemnly, a gesture of respect for battles fought both on stage and in the trenches of life.

"Indeed," Nate agreed, his posture relaxed but his mind razor-sharp, cataloging every reaction. Every story shared tightened the net of trust they cast around the group.

"Here's to new friends and old stories," Diane declared, lifting her mug in salute.

"Cheers," the group echoed, the word a pact sealed in red wine and determination.

As glasses met in the center of the circle, Nate and Amy's eyes locked briefly—a silent promise that they were only getting started.

Nate leaned against a prop table, his gaze casual but alert. Laughter bubbled from the cluster of actors nearby, their camaraderie genuine, or so it seemed. He watched as Sapphire, now dressed in his male attire and calling himself Stan, sidled up to one of the younger cast members engrossed in her phone. A glint of curiosity sparked in Stan's dark eyes as he peered over her shoulder, feigning interest in the photo on the screen.

"Nice shot," he murmured, his voice smooth. But Nate saw the flicker of something more—a relentless scrutiny masked by a smile too practiced.

Amy, meanwhile, found Diane in the wings, her presence a calming force amidst the bustle. Her voice was soft, yet deliberate. "Diane, these accidents lately... must be tough on everyone."

Diane's hand paused mid-fold on a costume she was tending to. She glanced up, her blue eyes clouded with concern. "It's been challenging, yes." Her words came slow, measured.

"Seems like bad luck has taken center stage," Amy probed gently, watching for the telltale signs of evasion or deceit.

"Sometimes I wonder if it's just bad luck or..." Diane trailed off, her gaze drifting.

"Or?" Amy encouraged, leaning in.

"Or if someone's pulling the strings," Diane admitted, her lips pressing into a thin line.

Nate caught the tail end of their conversation, his senses sharpening. Strings being pulled aligned all too well with the tension he sensed beneath the surface—Stan's watchful eye, the unnatural streak of misfortunes plaguing the group.

"Thanks, Diane. That's helpful to know," Amy said with a knowing wink, touching Diane's arm lightly before moving away.

Nate melded back into the crowd, ready to pull at the threads of this tangled mystery. Stan's suspicious behavior, Diane's veiled hints—it was a puzzle begging to be solved. And they were just the pair to do it.

Nate checked his watch. Amy caught his eye and nodded; it was time.

"Great work today, folks," Nate called out, clapping his hands for attention. "Can't wait to see what we do next time."

"Absolutely," Amy chimed in, her smile engaging as she waved to the departing members. "You're all amazing; this is going to be a fantastic show."

They exchanged handshakes and hugs with Diane, Martin, Cynthia, Susan, Robert, and even Sapphire, who offered a cautious smile. Nate's eyes lingered on her just a moment longer than necessary, storing away the image of her guarded expression.

"See you all soon!" Amy's voice echoed through the now-emptying space as they headed towards the door.

Once outside, the air crisp against their faces, they quickened their pace. A safe distance from the theater, they ducked into a dimly lit café that promised both privacy and strong coffee.

"Okay, debrief," Nate said, his voice low, as they settled into a secluded corner booth. "Sapphire slash Stan's shifty—caught him snooping on someone's socials."

"Could be nothing," Amy mused, but her furrowed brow suggested otherwise. "Or..."

"Or he's deeper in this than we thought," Nate finished, tapping a finger against his temple. "Diane's hinting at more than bad luck—it fits."

"Exactly." Amy leaned forward, her red hair falling over her shoulder like a curtain of focus. "We need more on this guy. And those 'strings' Diane mentioned? We pull at them, see what unravels."

"Right." Nate's gaze sharpened. "I'll do some digging online tonight. See what dirt comes up."

"Meanwhile, I'll compile our notes. Every interaction, every glance—we don't miss a beat."

"Good." Nate's lips curved into a determined half-smile. "Let's get to the bottom of this."

Amy's eyes sparked with resolve. "They won't see us coming."

Chapter 7

The theater lobby buzzed with anticipation, laughter and excited chatter filled the air as Nate and Amy stepped into the vibrant space. The scent of fresh paint and sawdust tickled their noses, hinting at the last-minute preparations for the upcoming production. Nate couldn't help but smile as he witnessed the enthusiasm that radiated from the theater group members.

"Feels like we're walking into a hive," Amy whispered, her eyes darting around to take everything in. Her instincts kicked in immediately, noting every detail and filing it away for later analysis.

"Let's dive in, shall we?" Nate suggested.

"Sounds good to me," Amy replied, already sensing that there was more to this story than met the eye.

They quickly immersed themselves in the activities of the theater group, attending rehearsals and offering their assistance wherever needed. Amy, with her keen eye for detail, gained the trust of the wardrobe department, helping with costume fittings and making small adjustments that improved both comfort and appearance. Her genuine interest in the actors' lives allowed her to blend seamlessly into their world, collecting information and establishing connections.

"Nice job on the alterations, Amy," one of the actresses complimented her. "I can actually breathe in this thing now!"

"Thanks, I'm just here to help," she replied with a warm smile, mentally adding another piece to the puzzle they were trying to solve.

Nate, meanwhile, put his hacking skills to use by assisting with the set-building process. As he worked alongside the crew, he carefully observed the interactions between the theater group members, watching for any signs of tension or discord. He noticed how some individuals seemed to be particularly protective of certain areas of the stage, as if guarding something valuable.

"Hey Nate, can you hand me that hammer?" a set-builder called out.

"Sure thing!" he replied, passing the tool and taking note of the man's body language. There was something going on beneath the surface, and Nate knew that uncovering it was the key to solving the mystery they had stumbled into.

***

Nate felt the floor vibrate beneath him as the actors danced and sang during the rehearsal. The energy in the room was palpable.

"Great job, everyone!" Amy exclaimed, clapping her hands along with the others. She had seamlessly slipped into the role of an enthusiastic theater enthusiast and was building connections with the group members.

"Isn't this exciting?" whispered a woman named Julie to Nate. "I can't believe opening night is only a week away."

"Absolutely," Nate responded, genuinely impressed by the performance he'd just witnessed. "You all have been working so hard; it's going to be amazing."

As they broke for a short intermission, Nate and Amy found themselves engaged in conversations with various members of the theater group.

"Have you heard about what's been happening to some of the cast members recently?" one performer asked, leaning closer to Amy. "It's terrible. Facebook profiles hacked, bank accounts drained... I don't know who would do such a thing to us."

"Really?" Amy replied, feigning surprise while mentally taking note of each incident that was mentioned. "That's awful."

"Seems like someone's out to get us," another actor chimed in. "But why? We're just a small community theater group."

"Maybe someone's jealous of your success," Nate suggested, his mind racing as he searched for a connection between the victims. He knew that identifying a pattern was crucial in figuring out who was behind these attacks.

"Could be," the actor agreed. "But we're not going to let them bring us down. We've worked too hard for this production."

"You shouldn't let anyone spoil your moment in the spotlight," Amy said with a supportive smile.

The stage lights cast a sharp, contrasting glow on Martin Brown's face as he applied the finishing touches to his make-up, his reflection in the mirror betraying a mixture of excitement and vulnerability. Amy approached him cautiously, careful not to disturb his focus.

"Hey, Martin," she said with a friendly smile. "You're looking great for tonight's performance."

"Thanks, Amy," he replied, his dark brown eyes meeting hers in the mirror. "Just trying to get into character, you know?"

"Of course," Amy nodded, her red hair catching the light as she leaned against the dressing table. "You are to your craft. It's truly inspiring."

"Ah, well, you know what they say: 'All the world's a stage,'" Martin chuckled before his expression turned somber. "Though, lately, it seems like someone's trying to take over the role of the villain around here."

"Really?" Amy asked gently, sensing his openness to share more about the recent identity thefts.

Meanwhile, Nate caught sight of Cynthia and Susan having an intense conversation near the wings of the stage. Their hushed voices, punctuated by angry gestures, hinted at hidden tensions within the group. He observed them closely, his instincts telling him that their exchange was important.

"Look, Cynthia," Susan whispered, her green eyes flashing with anger. "I don't know what you think you saw, but you're wrong. Just let it go."

"Let it go?" Cynthia snapped back, her blue eyes welling with tears. "How can I? I thought we were friends, Susan. But if you're not willing to stand up for us, then who will?"

"Keep your voice down," Susan hissed, glancing around to see if anyone was watching. "You don't know the whole story, so just stay out of it."

"Fine," Cynthia replied, wiping away her tears and storming off in the opposite direction.

Nate's brow furrowed as he considered the implications of their exchange. What had Cynthia seen, and why was Susan so determined to keep it quiet? He knew he needed to dig deeper into the theater group's dynamics to uncover the truth behind the recent misfortunes.

As Amy and Nate continued their investigation, they each felt a growing sense of urgency. Neither of them could shake the feeling that time was running out, and that if they didn't act soon, the curtain would fall on an even darker chapter for the theater group.

Nate's hands gripped a wooden plank as he helped with set-building, the sound of hammering echoing in the theater. The hustle and bustle of eager actors and crew members surrounded him, but his thoughts were consumed by the hidden tensions he'd observed within the group.

"Hey, Nate," called a fellow set-builder, snapping Nate out of his reverie. "Can you hand me that screwdriver?"

"Sure thing," Nate replied, passing the tool to his new acquaintance. As he leaned down to retrieve it, he noticed a small catch on the edge of the stage. Curiosity piqued, he inconspicuously slid the catch open, revealing a hidden compartment.

"Excuse me for a moment," Nate muttered to the set-builder. He crouched down, feeling his pulse quicken as he reached into the compartment. His fingers brushed against an assortment of personal items - wallets, keys, and even a small jewelry box.

Nate frowned, realizing that this discovery was far from innocent. The stolen identities, the drained bank accounts – it all seemed to lead back to this very spot. He carefully replaced the items and slid the catch shut, storing this revelation away in his mind for later discussion with Amy.

Meanwhile, Amy found herself among the costume racks, eavesdropping on a heated argument between Diane and Sapphire. She hid behind a row of vibrant dresses, her red hair blending with their flamboyant hues.

"Look, Diane, I understand you're concerned about the recent misfortunes," Sapphire snapped, her voice dripping with thinly veiled disdain. "But don't go pointing your finger at me when there's no proof."

"Proof?" Diane retorted, her kind blue eyes narrowing. "You've been acting suspiciously ever since these incidents started. And now, people are suffering because of it."

"Coincidence Darling," Sapphire replied coolly. "And if you think I'd be so careless as to leave any evidence lying around, then you're even more naive than I thought."

Amy's heart pounded in her chest. This argument confirmed her suspicions about Sapphire's involvement in the theater group's misfortunes. She knew she and Nate needed to act fast.

As the rehearsal continued, Nate and Amy exchanged a knowing glance, silently communicating their shared urgency. Their mission was clear: uncover the truth and protect the innocent before it was too late. But they also knew that the path ahead would be fraught with danger, and they would need to tread carefully to avoid becoming entangled in the web of deception themselves.

Nate stood still in the shadows, his eyes scanning the bustling theater group members as they prepared for another round of rehearsals. He gave Amy a subtle nod.

"Hey, Martin," Amy said casually. "I couldn't help but overhear some talk about recent unfortunate events affecting the group. What's been going on?"

Martin hesitated, glancing around nervously before leaning in closer. "Well, I probably shouldn't be talking about this, but several of us have had our identities stolen. My bank account was drained last week, and someone else had their Facebook profile hijacked." He rubbed his temples, clearly distressed. "The whole thing has put everyone on edge."

"Sounds terrible," Amy replied sympathetically. "Has anyone noticed anything... odd? Any strange behavior or suspicious characters?"

"Other than Sapphire?" Martin mumbled, raising an eyebrow. "Can't say I have. But then again, it's hard to trust anyone these days."

"True," Amy agreed, filing away the information. She knew better than to push too hard. A delicate touch was needed for such investigations.

Meanwhile, Nate chatted with Cynthia and Susan, the two women he had observed in a tense exchange earlier. As the conversation unfolded, he listened intently for any inconsistencies in their stories, searching for clues that might point to the mastermind behind the identity thefts.

"Hey, you two seem really close," Nate ventured, steering the conversation towards their relationship. "Have you ever had any disagreements or issues with other members?"

"Of course," Cynthia admitted, her voice tight. "We're like a family here, and families have their ups and downs. But we always work through it... eventually."

"Any recent issues?" Nate pressed, his dark eyes probing for any sign of deception.

"Nothing major," Susan answered evasively, shifting her weight from one foot to the other. "Just the usual drama that comes with putting on a show."

Nate's gut told him there was more to their story, but he knew better than to push too hard. For now, he would keep an eye on them.

During a break in the rehearsals, Nate and Amy rendezvoused backstage, exchanging the information they had gathered. As they spoke in hushed tones, Amy spotted a notebook tucked under a pile of stage props. She carefully pulled it free, revealing Sapphire's name scrawled across the front cover.

"Look what I've found," she whispered to Nate, who immediately recognized the potential significance of the discovery.

They quickly leafed through the pages, finding cryptic notes and suspicious-looking diagrams that seemed to allude to something sinister. Nate's fingers traced over the complex spiderweb of connections laid out before them, his mind racing to decipher the hidden meaning behind Sapphire's notations.

The stage lights cast dramatic shadows on the tense faces of the cast members as they rehearsed a particularly emotional scene. Nate and Amy, still immersed in their roles within the theater group, kept a close watch on the growing desperation etched in the expressions of their newfound friends. A palpable determination to uncover the truth behind the misfortunes plaguing them vibrated through the air.

"Something's not right," Nate muttered under his breath as he observed Cynthia furiously scribbling notes during a break in the rehearsal. He caught Amy's eye and they shared a knowing glance.

"Agreed," she whispered back, her gaze darting between the weary faces surrounding them. "They're all on edge, and it's only getting worse."

Nate's brow furrowed with concern as he considered their next move. As much as he wanted answers, he didn't want to put anyone at risk, especially those who had already fallen victim to the nefarious schemes unfolding around them. In a quiet corner backstage, he pulled Amy aside for a moment of reflection.

"Can we really do this, Amy?" Nate asked, his voice wavering with uncertainty. "Can we uncover the truth and protect everyone without putting ourselves or the others in danger?"

Amy hesitated, weighing the risks against the potential reward. She knew Nate was right – there were no guarantees that they could navigate this treacherous landscape unscathed. But she also couldn't shake the fierce protectiveness that surged within her, urging her to fight for justice.

"Look at them, Nate," she said softly, gesturing towards the anxious cast members. "These people have already suffered so much. If we don't try to help them, who will?"

Nate sighed, knowing Amy was right. They had come too far to turn back now. Steeling himself, he nodded in agreement.

"Alright," he conceded. "Let's do this. Together."

They returned to the bustling energy of the rehearsal, Nate and Amy shared a renewed sense of purpose in their mission. They knew the path ahead was fraught with danger, but they were determined to see it through – even if it meant putting everything on the line.

The stage lights flickered and cast eerie shadows on the walls, as the sound of a prop being knocked over echoed through the theater. Nate and Amy exchanged worried glances, their hearts pounding in unison with the heightened tension in the room.

"Places, everyone!" the director called out, his voice laced with unease. The actors hurried to their positions, their movements frantic and desperate, as if they were trying to outrun their own fear.

"Alright," Nate whispered to Amy, "let's keep our eyes peeled for anything suspicious. And remember, stay close."

As the rehearsal resumed, the couple observed the scene with hawk-like intensity, searching for any telltale signs of deception or treachery. But amidst the chaos, it was difficult to discern what was genuine emotion and what was merely a well-rehearsed façade.

"Did you see that?" Amy muttered under her breath, nodding toward Sapphire, who was whispering angrily into Diane's ear. "Seems like there's more going on behind the scenes than just the play."

"Definitely," Nate agreed, his mind racing as he tried to piece together the convoluted puzzle they had stumbled upon. "But let's not jump to conclusions yet. We need hard evidence before we can make any accusations."

As the final act began, the atmosphere in the theater grew increasingly tense. It was as if an invisible force was tightening its grip around them all, coiling like a snake waiting to strike.

Then, without warning, disaster struck.

"Stop!" Martin Brown, one of the actors, screamed, as he stumbled across the stage, clutching his chest. His face contorted in agony, and he collapsed onto the floor, gasping for breath.

"Martin!" Amy cried out, rushing to his side. Nate followed closely behind, scanning the room for any sign of foul play. The other actors stared in shock, frozen in place by the terrifying turn of events.

"Call an ambulance!" Nate shouted, as he assessed Martin's rapidly deteriorating condition. "Now!"

As Amy dialed emergency services, Nate couldn't shake the feeling that this was more than just a tragic accident – it was another piece in the twisted game they had unwittingly become entangled in.

"Is this really happening?" Amy asked, her voice trembling as she relayed the details to the dispatcher. "Or are we just seeing shadows where there aren't any?"

"Right now, I don't know," Nate admitted, his eyes never leaving the scene unfolding before them. "But one thing's for sure – we're not leaving until we get to the bottom of this."

As the sirens wailed in the distance, signaling the arrival of the paramedics, Nate and Amy exchanged a grim look of determination.

They knew that the stakes had just been raised, and there was no turning back now. The truth was out there, lurking in the darkness, and they would stop at nothing to bring it to light.

Chapter 8

Amy leaned against the paint-chipped wall, her gaze fixed on the stage where actors milled about, their voices a collage of lines and laughter. She took in each movement, every expression. Details mattered in her line of work—both on stage and off.

"Everhart," a voice called, breaking through the rehearsal's din.

She turned, red hair catching the light, to see Martin Brown approaching. The lead actor. His steps were deliberate, his dark eyes focused. A script clutched in one hand, evidence of his perpetual preparation.

"Brown," she replied, a playful edge to her tone. "Lost in your character again?"

"Always," he chuckled. "It's the only way to live on stage."

"Indeed." Amy nodded, folding her arms. She knew personas well—the ones she created were often more elaborate than any theater production could muster.

"Favorite play?" Martin asked, leaning beside her, close but not too close.

"Hard to choose," Amy said, her voice a lure. "But 'The Sting' has a certain appeal."

"Ah, a tale of con artists," Martin observed. "Fitting."

"Yours?" Amy watched him carefully, the exchange as much an assessment as it was a conversation.

"Shakespeare's 'Macbeth.' Ambition, tragedy, compelling characters," he listed, his passion tangible.

"Sounds like a recipe for disaster." Amy smirked, aware of the irony.

"Or success," Martin countered, his smile sharp, inviting challenge.

"Depends on who's playing the game," she quipped, her words tinged with double meaning.

"Indeed." Martin's eyes danced with amusement. "And how dedicated they are to winning."

"Careful," Amy teased, her gaze never wavering. "That kind of dedication can lead to madness. Or worse."

"Or brilliance," Martin shot back, his flirtation wrapped in confidence.

"Fine line," Amy conceded with a half-smile, her own commitment to detail mirroring his, though to a different end.

"Walk it with me?" Martin suggested, a hint of dare in his voice.

"Perhaps," Amy mused, the corners of her mouth turning up slightly. Their banter was a dance, and she was a skilled partner.

"Only if you can keep up," Martin added, the challenge set.

"Try me," Amy responded, her tone playful yet laced with the steel of her true nature.

Their laughter mingled, a shared moment amidst the backdrop of rehearsals—a scene set for intrigue and unexpected alliances.

Martin leaned against the stage, eyes fixed on Amy as the final lines of their rehearsal scene echoed off the walls. He straightened up, his gaze following her as she brushed a lock of fiery hair from her face.

"Hey," he said, once the director called a break. "Coffee after this? I want to hear more about your take on 'The Sting.'"

"Sure," Amy replied, a glint of intrigue in her eyes. "I have a few cons up my sleeve."

Their shared laughter was cut short by the sound of hammering from backstage. They glanced over to see Nate and Diane surrounded by half-built set pieces, their focus intent.

"Looks intense," Martin commented.

"Those two?" Amy's lips curled into a knowing smile. "They're probably swapping war stories."

Nate held a blueprint in one hand, a hammer in the other. His attention was on Diane, who recounted an ordeal with a faulty lighting rig that nearly brought a previous production to its knees. Her hands gestured wildly, mimicking the sparks that had flown.

"Sounds like a close call," Nate said, nodding his approval. "You've got guts."

"Comes with the territory," Diane replied. "What about you? Ever faced down a real villain?"

"More than I can count," Nate said with a wry grin. "Let's just say I'm not a fan of bullies."

"Justice seeker, huh?" Diane's eyes warmed with respect.

"Something like that." Nate's hammer struck true, a set piece firmly joined.

"Good." She smiled. "We need more of those."

In the wings, the stage lights flickered, signaling the end of the break. Amy turned back to Martin, the promise of coffee and conspiracy still hanging in the air.

"Later, then?" Martin asked.

"Later," Amy confirmed, her mind already racing ahead to the next act of their own elaborate con.

Sawdust peppered the air, the scent sharp and raw. Nate's hands worked with a habitual precision, fitting another panel into the skeletal set. His gaze shifted to Diane, who wiped a bead of sweat from her forehead.

"Didn't peg you for a craftsman," Diane said, her voice tinged with amusement.

"Army teaches you a few things," Nate replied, his movements never ceasing. "Resourcefulness is one."

"Army, huh?" Diane's interest piqued as she handed him a screw.

"Yep." He took it, locking the panel in place. "Learned more about people than warfare, honestly."

"Is that so?"

"Believe it or not, it's why I'm here. Helping out, laying low, making things right when I can." The last screw tightened, he straightened up, eyes meeting hers. "You?"

"Life's thrown its curveballs. But, like you, I believe in justice. In standing up when others can't." She brushed sawdust from her jeans, her stance firm and resolute.

"Sounds like we're cut from the same cloth," Nate said, a note of camaraderie in his tone.

"Seems that way." Diane nodded, her smile genuine.

Their shared laughter was brief but telling. As they returned to their task, the foundation of trust had been laid, piece by sturdy piece.

The clink of mugs set a rhythm to their conversation. Amy leaned across the table, her eyes alight with passion as she recounted an exposé that had nearly unraveled before it began. Martin mirrored her intensity, leaning in to catch every word.

"Undercover for months," Amy said, her voice low and steady. "It was like living in someone else's skin."

"Acting isn't so different," Martin replied, sipping his coffee. "You become another person entirely."

"Except my audience doesn't clap at the end. They either get locked up or walk free." Her lips quirked into a half-smile.

"High stakes." Martin nodded, respect etched into his features.

"Always." She tilted her head. "But it's about the truth, isn't it? Uncovering lies, revealing secrets."

"Exactly," he agreed, setting his mug down. "There's honesty in a performance, even through fiction."

"Life's greatest paradox," she mused. Their laughter filled the space, warm and genuine.

Hours slipped by unnoticed as personal tales wove together with dreams yet to unfold. It wasn't just coffee they shared but parts of themselves, each revelation another scene in a play with an unknown ending.

***

Nate and Diane walked, the rhythm of their steps a silent language. Parks became their stage, open skies their backdrop. Time outside the theater blurred the lines between roles and reality.

"Never thought I'd find someone who gets it," Nate admitted, hands buried in his jacket pockets.

"Likewise." Diane's breath formed clouds in the chill air. "Most people don't understand what it takes to keep going."

"Or why we do it." He glanced over, catching the determined glint in her eye.

"Exactly." She pulled her scarf tighter. "Justice has its own pull."

"Right you are," Nate said. Shared meals stitched their days together, each bite a testament to a growing kinship.

"Feels good, doesn't it?" Diane asked one evening, as they shared a bench, watching dusk claim the day.

"Having someone on your side?" Nate considered the question, weighing the comfort against the risk. "Yeah, it does."

Their bond solidified with every story and silenced moment. Side by side, they weren't just comrades; they were guardians of a cause, a companionship forged in adversity and trust.

*****

Amy flipped through her script, the pages whispering secrets of a life she was pretending to embrace. Martin hovered nearby, his presence a gravitational pull she found hard to ignore.

"Missed your mark," he teased, pointing to a spot on the stage. His voice carried easily, infused with the warmth that had kept them talking until the stars blinked out.

Laughter trickled from the wings where the theater group huddled, their eyes darting between Amy and Martin like spectators at a tennis match. The air crackled with unspoken jokes and knowing looks; their flirtation wasn't just text between lines now—it was the headline.

"Guess I'm distracted," she volleyed back, eyes meeting his in a challenge.

"By what, I wonder?" He smirked, stepping into her space, the exchange sparking another round of chuckles from their audience.

Across the room, Nate leaned against a freshly painted set piece, watching Diane as she brushed strokes of vermillion onto a prop. Her smile was evidence enough—warmth bloomed there, a rare flower nurtured by shared confidences.

"Careful," Nate called out, a hint of steel beneath the concern as a ladder wobbled near Diane. He moved without thought, a protector by instinct, steadying the metal frame before danger could claim its due.

"Thanks," she said, her gratitude reaching him even amidst the cacophony of rehearsals. Her gaze held his for a moment longer than necessary, an unspoken acknowledgment passing between them.

The other members took note—their whispers weaving a subtext into the fabric of the scene. Diane's smile, Nate's watchful eye; it told a story of camaraderie growing into something more profound.

As the director clapped for attention, the actors returned to their marks, but the undercurrent of their connections remained. Amy and Martin shared a glance, electric and loaded with promise. Nate positioned himself with a clear view of Diane, ready to intervene should fate misstep.

In this world of make-believe, the lines of reality were blurring, and the truth of their bond was taking center stage.

Nate scanned the auditorium, his gaze sharp. The stage lights cast long shadows, hiding secrets in plain sight. He caught Amy's eye, a silent signal exchanged. They were deep undercover, their playful banter with Diane and Martin a cover for something darker. Justice was the endgame, and this theater—its cast unknowingly entangled in a wealthy benefactor's corrupt web—was their current chessboard.

Amy laughed at something Martin said, her red hair catching the spotlight's glint. To anyone else, she was just an actress, engrossed in her role. But beneath the veneer, her mind was a whir of strategy. Every gesture, every word, calculated. She'd seen firsthand what injustice could do. Her father's empty chair at the dinner table was a daily reminder.

"Stay sharp," Nate murmured to himself, eyes flicking to the exits, the darkened corners where threats might lurk. He remembered too well the cost of distraction. In the military, a moment's lapse could mean life or death. Here, on this different battlefield, it meant the difference between exposing the guilty and becoming another casualty in their game.

The rehearsal wrapped, bodies milling about, the energy of ending scenes still vibrating in the air. Amy found herself alone with Martin, the others filtering out, leaving them isolated in the wings. Their eyes met, and the world narrowed to the space between them.

Elsewhere, Nate found Diane packing away props. Her hands, strong yet gentle, cradled a fragile mask, setting it down with care. He approached, his shadow merging with hers. "Let me help," he offered, voice low.

"Thank you, Nate," Diane replied, turning to face him. Her eyes shone with unspoken understanding. He reached out, his fingers brushing hers as they lifted a backdrop together.

Chapter 9

Nate and Amy sat in their makeshift headquarters, a rented storage unit filled with whiteboards, charts, and an assortment of computer monitors. The dim lighting flickered above them as they poured over the evidence they'd gathered so far on Sapphire's identity theft scheme.

"Look at this," Nate said, tapping the screen of his laptop. "I've been going through the stolen data and found a pattern. Sapphire targets theater group members who have recently come into some money – inheritance, lottery winnings, that sort of thing."

Amy leaned in for a closer look, her red hair cascading over her shoulder. "That makes sense. Vulnerable, and likely inexperienced with large sums of money. Easy pickings for someone like Sapphire."

"Exactly," Nate agreed, a hint of anger rippling beneath his calm expression. He hated seeing innocent people being taken advantage of, especially those who had already experienced hardship.

"Alright, let's see if we can track down any of Sapphire's digital footprints," he said, cracking his knuckles before setting to work on the keyboard. His fingers flew across the keys, the clicks and clacks melding together into a rhythmic dance.

Amy watched him work, always amazed by the way Nate could navigate the digital world with such ease. She knew he used his hacking skills for good now, but she couldn't help but be impressed by his sheer talent.

"Got something," Nate announced triumphantly. "I found an IP address that seems to be connected to the stolen data. And check this out." He clicked on a series of icons, revealing a web of email accounts and social media profiles linked to the same address.

"Good work!" Amy praised, her eyes scanning the information displayed on the screen. "Now we just need to cross-reference this with the victims' personal data and see if we can establish a connection."

"Already on it," Nate replied, a wry smile playing on his lips. He admired Amy's tenacity and attention to detail, qualities that made them an unstoppable team.

As they worked late into the night, piecing together the puzzle of Sapphire's identity theft scheme, Nate felt a sense of pride in their mission. Together, they were determined to bring justice to those who preyed on the vulnerable, no matter how elaborate the con. And with each new discovery, they grew closer to exposing Sapphire's true motives and methods.

***

The first rays of morning light crept through the blinds as Amy hunched over her laptop, sifting through Sapphire's past like an archaeologist uncovering ancient ruins. Nate had done his part in the digital realm; now it was her turn to dig deeper. As an investigative journalist, she knew the importance of understanding a story from all angles. And with Sapphire, there were more angles than a geometry textbook.

"Anything interesting?" Nate asked, rubbing sleep from his eyes and refilling his coffee mug.

"Stanley Richards, aka Sapphire, has quite the history," Amy replied, her eyes never leaving the screen. "A few arrests for petty theft and fraud, but nothing that would have landed him in serious trouble. However, I did find some connections to known criminals involved in identity theft."

"Sounds like we're getting closer," Nate said, taking a sip of his coffee. "What's our next move?"

"We need eyes on Sapphire," Amy declared, closing her laptop with determination. "We need to catch him in the act if we want to expose his scheme and help the theater group members."

***

Nate and Amy arrived at the theater group's rehearsal space, armed with state-of-the-art, unobtrusive, surveillance equipment. As they entered the dimly lit room, the scent of sweat and stage makeup hung heavy in the air, a reminder of the countless hours spent perfecting performances.

"Let's set up cameras near the dressing rooms and the backstage area," Amy suggested, her mind racing with possibilities. "Those seem like prime spots for stealing personal information."

"Good thinking," Nate agreed. He expertly positioned each camera to capture every angle. He had come a long way from hacking for fun, but the thrill of outsmarting the enemy still coursed through his veins.

As they finished setting up the surveillance equipment, Amy felt a slight twinge of guilt. These theater group members had welcomed them with open arms, and now they were spying on them to catch a thief in their midst. But she knew that sometimes, the path to justice required stepping into the shadows.

"Are you ready for this?" Nate asked, sensing Amy's hesitation.

"Of course," she replied, her resolve hardening like steel. "Let's bring Sapphire's identity theft scheme to light."

With the cameras in place, Nate and Amy retreated to their makeshift surveillance hub, eyes glued to the screens as they waited for any signs of suspicious behavior from Sapphire. The stakes were high, but together, they were a force to be reckoned with - a dynamic duo determined to protect the vulnerable and expose corruption at any cost.

***

Nate logged into fakenamegenerator.com and created a new online persona. After generating personal details, he went to thispersondoesnotexist.com and grabbed a suitable photo for his newly created persona.

"Mandy" was young, naive, and eager to please - the perfect bait for Sapphire's identity theft scheme. Clicking "submit" on Mandy's newly created social media profiles, he felt a swell of satisfaction at the prospect of outsmarting their cunning adversary.

"Alright, Mandy's all set up," Nate announced to Amy, who had been scouring the internet for any additional information on Sapphire. "Let's see if this gets Sapphire's attention."

"Good work," Amy said, buzzing with anticipation. "Now we just need to make sure the rest of the theater group is aware of what's going on."

"Yes," Nate replied, his tone serious as he considered the potential consequences for their newfound friends. "We need to have a meeting with everyone."

Amy nodded in agreement, then reached for her phone to send out a group text. Within minutes, they'd arranged for an urgent gathering at the rehearsal space the following day.

***

As the theater group members filed into the room, Nate could sense their curiosity and concern. He glanced at Amy, who gave him an encouraging nod. Taking a deep breath, he began to speak.

"Thank you all for coming on such short notice," Nate started, addressing the room with authority. "We've uncovered some disturbing information about a member of our group, and we need your help."

The room buzzed with murmurs and sideways glances, but Nate pressed on. "Someone has been stealing the personal information of our fellow theater members and using it for their own nefarious purposes.."

The shock was palpable, but Nate and Amy continued, explaining their surveillance efforts and their plan to bait the thief with the fake online persona. As they spoke, Amy studied the faces of the group members, trying to gauge their reactions and spot any potential allies or adversaries.

"Please," Nate implored, his voice filled with genuine concern, "take care of your personal information. Change your passwords somewhat regularly, use a password manager and avoid using the same password elsewhere. Be sure to use multi-factor authentication wherever possible. If you have any questions about any of that, please talk to me afterwards. Be cautious with whom you share your details, and keep an eye out for any suspicious activity."

"Remember," Amy added, her red hair blazing like a battle flag as she stood alongside her partner, "we're all in this together. If we work as a team, we can expose the thief's true intentions and protect our theater family from further harm."

"Remember, it's vital to have different passwords for each account," she advised a young actress, her tone patient yet firm. "That's where a password manager really helps. And try to use a combination of letters, numbers, and symbols. Most password managers will be able to create a password for you. The only password that you should know is the one for the password manager."

"Got it," the young woman replied, nodding earnestly.

Nate couldn't help but feel a twinge of pride as he watched his wife in action, her instincts and skills blending seamlessly with her natural empathy. Yet, beneath his admiration, an undercurrent of urgency pulsed through him. They needed to catch Sapphire before their antagonist struck again.

As the evening wore on, Nate and Amy continued working with the theater group members, answering questions and dispensing advice. Each interaction was punctuated by the knowledge that any one of these people could be Sapphire's next target—or worse, an unwitting accomplice in the identity theft scheme.

"Keep an eye out for any unusual activity on your accounts," Nate told a nervous-looking actor, his voice steady and reassuring. "If anything seems off, contact your bank immediately and please let us know."

"Will do," the actor promised, clapping Nate on the shoulder before departing.

"Listen up," Nate announced to the gathered group, who stared back at him with wide, anxious eyes. "We're here to help you. We'll provide you with the necessary resources and support to recover from what Stanley's done and ensure it doesn't happen again."

"First things first," Amy chimed in, her tone reassuring yet firm. "You need to report the crimes to the proper authorities. Here's a list of agencies where you can file your complaints and access legal assistance if needed."

As Nate handed out the information sheets, he could see the relief washing over the group members' faces. They had been through so much, and now they finally had a chance to regain control of their lives.

"Additionally," Amy continued, "we'll help you strengthen your online security measures. Things like enabling two-factor authentication, regularly changing passwords, and being cautious of suspicious emails or messages are crucial to protecting yourselves."

"Remember," Nate added, "knowledge is power, and we're going to arm you with everything you need to stay safe and secure."

The theater group members nodded, determination replacing fear on their faces. And as they began the process of rebuilding their lives, Nate and Amy knew they had made a difference – not just by bringing down a criminal but by empowering those who had been victimized.

Chapter 10

The stage lights flickered, casting shadows on the motley crew of actors and actresses as they performed their lines with dramatic flair. Nate and Amy stood at the back of the theater, blending into the darkness, their eyes trained on Sapphire's every move.

"Stanley Richards is a chameleon," Nate muttered under his breath, watching as Sapphire effortlessly slipped into character. "I can see why he's been so hard to pin down."

"Looks like we've got our work cut out for us," Amy whispered, her fingers tapping anxiously against her thigh. The couple had spent countless hours poring over documents and hacking into online accounts in order to uncover Sapphire's true identity and expose his elaborate con. Now that they were finally face-to-face with their target, the stakes felt higher than ever.

During a break in the rehearsal, Nate spotted an opportunity. Sapphire sauntered over to a group of performers huddled around a laptop, engaging them in casual conversation while simultaneously peeking at the screen. Nate recognized the telltale signs of shoulder surfing - a tactic used by identity thieves to steal passwords and other sensitive information by simply watching as someone types it in.

"Gotcha," Nate murmured, discreetly raising his iPhone and snapping a series of photos that captured Sapphire in the act. He knew it was vital to gather concrete evidence of Sapphire's criminal activities if they were to have any hope of bringing him to justice. So much for him feeling remorseful and ceasing his nefarious activities.

"Nice catch," Amy whispered, impressed by her husband's quick thinking. As an investigative journalist, she had learned the importance of capturing the right moment, and Nate had done just that.

Nate allowed himself a small grin, but his thoughts were already racing ahead, calculating their next move. This was only the beginning of their mission, and they both knew there would be many more challenges ahead before they could unmask Sapphire and put an end to his dangerous game.

"Stay sharp, Amy," Nate warned, his voice low and serious. "This is far from over."

Amy's eyes narrowed as she watched Martin Brown glide across the stage, his every movement a testament to his dedication to the craft. She knew that getting close to him would be key to unraveling more of Sapphire's mysterious background and motivations.

"Quite the performance, isn't it?" Amy remarked casually, sidling up beside Martin during a break in rehearsal. Her heart raced with anticipation, but her voice remained steady, betraying none of her true intentions.

"Thank you," Martin replied, flashing her a charming smile as he wiped sweat from his brow. "It's been a labor of love."

"Speaking of love," Amy ventured, delicately broaching the subject of Sapphire. "Stanley seems quite enamored with the theater group. How did he get involved?"

Martin's expression softened as he recalled the first time he'd met Stanley, aka Sapphire. "He just appeared one day, offering to help with costumes and makeup. He's got an incredible talent for it."

"Does he have a background in theater production?" Amy pressed.

"Hard to say," Martin admitted, rubbing the back of his neck. "Stanley's always been a bit of an enigma. But he's become somewhat indispensable to the group."

"Indeed," Amy murmured, filing the information away for later analysis.

Meanwhile, Nate mingled with other members of the theater group, picking up tidbits of information about Sapphire's interactions with them. The more he learned, the more convinced he became that they were dealing with someone who had mastered the art of manipulation.

"Hey, check this out," one actor said to Nate, showing him a brand new debit card. "Sapphire helped me set up a bank account for my costume expenses."

"Really?" Nate feigned interest, his mind racing. "That's very generous of him."

"Definitely," the actor agreed, oblivious to Nate's inner turmoil and having already forgotten the meeting 2 days ago.

Just then, Nate's keen eyes caught Sapphire entering the costume room. He nudged Amy and subtly nodded in that direction, signaling her to follow him.

As they peered into the room, they saw Sapphire gently handling someone's debit card, deftly snapping a photo of it with his phone before returning it to its rightful place. Nate's hand tensed around his own iPhone, cursing himself for not being able to capture this moment as he had done earlier.

"Did you see that?" Amy whispered, her voice barely audible.

"I did," Nate replied, clenching his jaw. "We need to gather more evidence and expose him publicly before it's too late."

Amy nodded, her determination renewed. Together, they withdrew from the doorway, their minds racing with plans to finally bring Sapphire's elaborate con to an end.

***

Nate's fingers danced across the keyboard, his eyes locked on the screen. His mind was a whirlwind, his focus razor-sharp as he unveiled Sapphire's digital footprint. Infiltrating the fake Facebook account proved to be a challenge, but Nate was nothing if not persistent.

"Gotcha," he muttered, finally gaining access. What he found made his blood run cold – a web of connections to other theater group members, all potential victims of identity theft. A tangled mess of lies and manipulation that only served to confirm their suspicions about Sapphire.

"Any luck?" Amy asked, her voice tinged with concern. She had been pacing nervously behind him, anxiously waiting for any new information they could use against their adversary.

"Definitely," Nate replied, his voice strained. "But we need to act fast."

***

Nate couldn't shake a nagging sense of unease, which grew heavier with every passing moment. He glanced around the room, his gaze falling on Diane, who seemed to be lost in thought. Seizing the opportunity to confide in her, he approached her cautiously.

"Hey, Diane," he said softly, his voice betraying the weight of his worries.

"Hello, Nate," Diane responded warmly, her eyes meeting his with genuine concern. "What's troubling you, dear?"

Nate hesitated for a moment, then let out a deep breath. "It's just... everything we've uncovered about Sapphire, and how many people are at risk. I can't help but feel overwhelmed by the responsibility of it all."

Diane's expression softened, her motherly instincts kicking in. She placed a comforting hand on his shoulder, her touch soothing the storm of emotions within him.

"Listen," she said gently, "I know it's a lot to take in and handle. But remember, you're not alone in this fight. You've got Amy by your side, and we're all here to support you."

Nate felt the weight lifting ever so slightly and offered Diane a grateful smile. "Thank you, Diane. Your words mean more than you know."

"Anytime, dear," she replied, squeezing his shoulder reassuringly.

Amy stood in the dimly lit corridor, her back against the cold brick wall as she tried to catch her breath. The emotional turmoil that accompanied their investigation threatened to consume her, leaving her feeling overwhelmed and vulnerable.

"Are we really doing the right thing?" she whispered to herself, her gaze fixed on the worn floor beneath her feet. "Can I even handle this?"

Nate found Amy in the shadows, his brow furrowed with concern. "Hey, you okay?" he asked gently, placing a hand on her shoulder.

"Of course," Amy replied, forcing a smile that didn't quite reach her eyes. "Just... thinking."

"About what?" Nate pressed, sensing her unease.

"Everything we've uncovered..." Amy admitted, her voice trembling. "It's starting to feel like too much. What if we can't stop Sapphire? What if we're risking everything for nothing?"

Nate wrapped his arm around her, pulling her close. "We'll find a way," he assured her, his voice steady and determined. "We always do, remember? And we won't let anyone else get hurt."

Amy leaned into him, drawing strength from his unwavering belief in their mission. But as they stood there, an idea began to take shape in her mind – a plan that might just give them the edge they needed to expose Sapphire once and for all.

"Wait," she said suddenly, pulling away from Nate. "I think I know what we need to do."

"Go on," Nate urged, his eyes filled with curiosity.

"Remember how Sapphire took a photo of someone's debit card during that costume fitting? We could use that to our advantage," Amy explained, excitement building in her voice. "We stage a similar situation, make it look like I've carelessly left my wallet out. If we can catch him red-handed, we'll have all the evidence we need."

"Could work," Nate agreed, "but it's risky."

"True," Amy acknowledged, her heart pounding heavy in her chest. "But if we don't act soon, he'll continue to exploit these people. We owe it to them to try."

Nate studied her for a moment, weighing the risks against the potential rewards. Finally, he nodded. "Alright, let's do it. But we have to be careful. One wrong move and we're done for."

As they made their way back inside, Amy tried to shake off the lingering doubts that threatened to undermine her resolve. This was their chance to make a difference, to protect those who couldn't protect themselves.

"Ready?" Nate asked, his eyes filled with determination.

"Ready," Amy replied.

***

The dim glow of Nate's laptop screen cast eerie shadows on his face, as he hunched over the keyboard, tapping away furiously. Amy watched him from the edge of their hotel bed, her fingers worrying the sheets, and her mind racing with the implications of their plan.

"Got it," Nate murmured, his eyes flicking over lines of text. "An email exchange between Sapphire and his accomplice."

"Anything we can use?" Amy asked, leaning in to study the screen.

"Looks like they're planning a bit of a spree during the theater group's upcoming tour," Nate explained. "They'll have access to even more potential victims while they're traveling. Good opportunity for pickpocketing too."

"Those poor people won't know what hit them," Amy said, anger boiling inside her. She clenched her fists, "we can't let that happen."

"Agreed." Nate's voice was steel, though his eyes betrayed a hint of uncertainty. "But we need to tread carefully. If we slip up, it could all be for nothing."

Amy glanced across the room, where Martin's number was scribbled on a piece of paper.

"About Martin..." she hesitated, looking back at Nate. "I think I need to distance myself from him."

"Are you sure?" Nate asked, concern etching across his features. "He might be a valuable source of information."

"I know, but..." Amy sighed, her chest tightening with the weight of her decision. "His feelings for me could compromise everything we've worked for. It's too risky."

Nate studied her for a moment before nodding solemnly. "Alright. If you think it's for the best, I trust your judgment."

"Thanks," she whispered, a bittersweet ache settling in her chest.

Later that evening, Amy forced a smile as she approached Martin outside the theater. His face lit up when he saw her, and she felt a twinge of regret.

"Hey, Martin," she said, keeping her tone casual. "I just wanted to let you know that I won't be able to hang out as much. Things are getting really busy for me outside the group."

"Really?" Martin's disappointment was palpable. "That's too bad. I was hoping we could spend more time together."

"Me too," she murmured, "but maybe after all this is over, we can catch up?"

"Sure," Martin agreed, though his eyes were clouded with confusion and hurt. "Take care, Amy."

"Thanks." As she walked back towards Nate, she promised herself that they would bring Sapphire down – no matter the personal cost.

Chapter 11

Sapphire's fingers danced across his phone screen, the light tapping barely audible above the hum of backstage activity. His eyes flickered with a hint of paranoia as he installed Telegram, an icon of a paper airplane now nestled among myriad apps designed to conceal and deceive. He hunched over the device, ensuring prying eyes could not glimpse the encrypted messages that began to populate the chat list.

"New routine today," Sapphire typed briskly, his message disappearing into the digital ether seconds after it was read.

Nate leaned against a shadowed wall, his gaze sharp and observant. He watched Sapphire's every move, the subtle shift in behavior not lost on him. The once flamboyant and careless antagonist now wrapped himself in a cloak of caution so tight it practically screamed guilt.

"He's switched to encrypted comms," Nate murmured, just loud enough for Amy to catch.

"Means we're getting to him," Amy replied, her lips curving into a determined smile. She adjusted a prop nearby, her fingers brushing against the surface with feigned casualness while her mind raced with strategy.

The duo slipped further into their roles, mirroring the actors around them, their presence as natural as the worn floorboards beneath their feet. They shared knowing glances, coded messages in the tilt of a head or the flicker of an eye.

"Stay close to him, but not too close," Nate instructed, his voice a low thrum that matched the intensity of his focus.

"Sure," Amy shot back, her confidence unwavering.

Sapphire, meanwhile, altered his path through the theater like a man rewriting his own map. He took different hallways, lingered in unusual spots, avoided his usual haunts. Each deviation was a breadcrumb, and Nate and Amy were the persistent birds trailing behind, unseen yet ever-present.

"Let's split up," Nate suggested, his frame blending seamlessly with the ebb and flow of bodies moving around the stage. "Cover more ground."

"Got it," Amy agreed, her red hair a fiery streak as she moved in the opposite direction, her senses heightened, cataloging every change in pattern, every hesitant step Sapphire took.

They were hunters, methodical and relentless. The prey had sensed the pursuit, yet couldn't shake the shadows that clung to his every move. Sapphire's facade of control was cracking, and Nate and Amy were poised to slip through the fissures, ready to expose the truth hidden beneath layers of deceit.

With each encrypted message sent, each altered route taken, Sapphire unknowingly wove the net that would entangle him. And Nate and Amy were there, silently tightening the knots.

****

Diane's fingers drummed a staccato rhythm on the wooden armrest of her chair, mirroring the beat of suspicion pulsating through the group. In the dim backstage area, hushed voices traded theories like contraband goods.

"Have you noticed how jumpy everyone is?" whispered Tom, the prop master, his eyes darting around as though expecting shadows to leap into the light.

"Something's off," agreed Janet, the costume designer, pulling her shawl tighter around her shoulders as if warding off a chill or maybe the truth.

"Too many accidents, too many mistakes lately," murmured Greg, who handled lighting. "It's not just bad luck."

Alliances formed in quiet nods and knowing glances. They clustered together, their shared paranoia a new bond stronger than any script could provide.

Diane watched from her corner, her gaze fixed on Sapphire, who stood apart from the gatherings. He paced, phone in hand, a man enacting a private play. His movements were deliberate, a choreography of evasion. Diane noted the way he avoided eye contact, the way his laughter didn't quite reach his eyes.

She moved closer, feigning interest in a nearby costume rack. Her blue eyes, usually warm pools of comfort, sharpened with detective-like scrutiny. She observed the tension in Sapphire's shoulders, the quick glances over his shoulder, the furtive taps on his encrypted messenger app.

"Careful, Stan," she muttered under her breath, using Sapphire's lesser-known name, a reminder of the man beneath the makeup.

Diane's heart pounded, the beats an echo of the risks they all faced. The theater was a family, and now it seemed there was a wolf in their midst. She would watch, wait, and when the time came, expose the threat. For the sake of the group, for the sake of what they had built together, she couldn't let the discord fester.

"Trouble brews," she whispered to herself, a silent vow to cut through the maze of deception. The curtain was rising on a scene of intrigue, and Diane had stepped into the role of an unwitting investigator. Sapphire's next act would be under her vigilant gaze.

***

Martin's stride carried a purpose as he cornered Sapphire backstage, his tone hushed but intense. "People are talking, Stan. They're scared, and it's about you."

Sapphire, applying a streak of rouge with steady hands, met Martin's gaze in the mirror. "Fear is often misplaced, darling," he said smoothly, the picture of calm. "I'm no boogeyman."

"Then why all the secrets?" Martin pressed, his eyes searching Sapphire's reflection for a crack, a slip.

"Art thrives on mystery." Sapphire turned, a smile playing on his lips. "Wouldn't you agree?"

Martin faltered, the actor in him recognizing the diversion tactic. He backed off, the confrontation dissolving into the charged air.

***

Across the room, Nate caught Amy's eye, a silent signal exchanged. It was time to weave their narrative into the growing tapestry of distrust. As they mingled among the crew, their whispers were like a magician's sleight of hand—subtle, misdirecting.

"Stan's been jittery," Nate murmured to a grip, clapping him on the back. "You seen him?"

"Encrypted messages, too," Amy added elsewhere, her voice carrying just enough to be overheard by a passing costume designer.

With each planted seed, the suspicion rooted deeper, sprouting a garden of doubt around Sapphire. Nate and Amy moved through the crowd, invisible puppeteers tugging strings, crafting a stage where Sapphire would soon find himself spotlighted—not as the star, but as the suspect.

***

The theater was a hive of whispers, Diane leading the charge. She sifted through props, her eyes narrow, determined to find something, anything. Costumes were flipped inside out, scripts scanned for notes. The group was no longer just an ensemble; they were sleuths in their own right.

"Look here." One pointed at a schedule pinned to the wall, shifts and timings realigned, a pattern emerging. "Always around when things go missing."

"Could be nothing," another mused, but hope flickered in their eyes. They needed it to be something.

Nate watched, his gaze sharp as flint. He leaned close to Amy, their heads almost touching. "Time to nudge them further."

"Leave it to me," she whispered back, slipping away with a dancer's grace.

She paused by a desk, fingers dancing across it as if by accident. A USB drive 'forgotten' in plain sight. It was innocent enough, yet loaded with breadcrumbs—emails, doctored ledgers, all roads leading to Sapphire.

Nate circled back, feigning interest in a lighting cue sheet while he dropped a burner phone behind a stack of set blueprints. It chimed with messages that would never be traced back to him, all encrypted, all suspiciously timed.

"Find something?" he asked Diane, who had returned to the fray, holding up the USB like a trophy.

"Maybe," she said, eyes alight with the thrill of the chase. "This could be big."

"Or it could be a dead end," Nate cautioned, but his heart raced. The seed was planted, the doubt watered. Now they just had to wait for it to grow.

***

Sapphire's gaze darted across the rehearsal space, a place once vibrant with camaraderie now tainted by distrust. The whispers between actors seemed louder, their laughter too forced. He moved through the crowd like a shadow detaching itself from the walls, his once-magnetic charm reduced to a cold barrier.

"Stanley," someone called, but he ignored it. Sapphire only. Stanley was vulnerable; Sapphire was not.

"Is everything alright?" Diane asked, her eyes narrowed with concern—or was it suspicion?

"Never better," Sapphire lied, the words brittle on his tongue.

He retreated to the wings, watching from the darkness as Nate and Amy ran lines with an ease that made the rest of the theater troupe seem amateurish. How effortlessly they blended in, how seamlessly they had woven themselves into the fabric of his domain. It irked him.

Nate's laugh boomed across the stage, Amy's smile infectious. To everyone else, they were just another couple lost in the art. But Sapphire wasn't everyone else. He saw the slight nods, the coded glances. They were up to something.

In the middle of a heated scene, Sapphire interrupted the flow. "Stop!" His voice cut through the dialogue, silencing the room.

All eyes turned to him as he strode onto the stage, the lights casting long shadows behind him. He pointed an accusing finger at Nate and Amy. "You two," he spat out. "Thieves among us."

The accusation hung in the air, heavy and sharp. Nate's brow furrowed, the hint of a smirk playing on his lips. Amy remained calm, her gaze steady.

"Quite the performance, Sapphire," Nate said, stepping closer. "Not just a Queen, but a Drama Queen."

Amy produced a folder from her bag, tossing it at Sapphire's feet. It fanned open, revealing a web of evidence—emails, transactions—all pointing back to him.

"Care to explain this?" Amy challenged, arms crossed.

Sapphire's heart pounded. He skimmed the papers, his mind racing. Fake, all of it. But convincing. Too convincing. His eyes flicked up to meet theirs, a silent war waged in the look they exchanged.

"Forgery," he said at last, his voice a mix of defiance and unease.

"Or truth," Nate countered. "Hard to tell these days, isn't it?"

They stood there, locked in a battle of wills, while the theater group murmured amongst themselves. Sapphire knew he was cornered, but he wouldn't let them see him falter. Not now, not ever.

Sapphire straightened his spine, the spotlight warm on his face. His heart drummed a manic rhythm, but he summoned his most disarming smile. "Ladies, gentlemen, please," he implored, gesturing with open hands to the murmuring crowd. "We're all friends here, aren't we?"

He turned slowly, making eye contact with the theater group members, each nod and whisper fueling his performance. "Nate, Amy," he addressed them, "you've been with us for only a short time, yet you cast such wild accusations."

Nate stepped forward, the muscles in his jaw tensing. "We're looking for the truth, Sapphire. That's all."

Amy remained unyielding beside him, her eyes like steel traps. "And we'll find it," she added.

"Truth?" Sapphire chuckled, though it sounded hollow even to his own ears. "Or is this an attempt to undermine our trust? To sow discord among us?"

The room's energy shifted, tension crackling like static. Members of the group glanced at each other, uncertainty taking root.

Nate's eyes narrowed. "We don't play games, Sapphire. You know that."

"Games?" Sapphire echoed, feigning hurt. "I would never. But can we say the same for you two?"

He saw doubt flicker in a few gazes, felt the balance waver. He pressed on. "Consider who stands to gain from such chaos."

"Nobody gains from lies and deception," Amy retorted sharply. "Except the one weaving them."

A murmur of agreement rose from the group. Sapphire's grip on the situation was slipping, his efforts to pit them against the interlopers faltering.

"Think about it," Nate urged the others, his voice carrying weight, conviction. "Look at the facts."

"Exactly," Sapphire snapped back. "Facts. Not concocted evidence meant to frame someone."

"Concocted?" Amy challenged, stepping into the fray. "Or meticulously gathered, pointing to a single source?"

"Enough!" Sapphire shouted, his facade cracking. "This is my stage, and I won't be upstaged by amateurs!"

"Then prove us wrong," Nate said, his tone cool and steady. "Clear your name."

"Clear..." For a moment, Sapphire was speechless. The challenge was direct, undeniable.

He knew then that Nate and Amy wouldn't budge, their resolve as solid as the stage beneath their feet. They were relentless, steadfast protectors of the innocent they sought to defend. And in that instant, Sapphire realized he was playing to an audience that had already judged him.

"Very well," he said, his voice low, eyes darting across the faces before him. "Let this be the final act."

The room pulsed with tension, a silent crescendo that reached every corner. Theater group members exchanged glances, the weight of the revelations tugging at the seams of their unity. Some bit their lips; others folded arms, forming barriers to shield themselves from the discomfort of doubt.

"Can't be." Diane muttered, her voice barely above a whisper, laced with betrayal. Her eyes, usually glued to Sapphire's for cues, now darted away, evading the dark pools that once commanded her trust.

Martin paced the length of the stage, his footsteps echoing like distant thunder. He stopped and faced Sapphire, the internal conflict clear on his furrowed brow. "Years... we've followed your lead," he said, the words heavy, reluctant, as if dragging them up was tearing him apart.

Sapphire stood center stage, a figure diminished, the spotlight exposing rather than flattering. The air of sophistication had evaporated, replaced by a palpable unease that clung to him like a second skin.

"Justice," a voice called out, firm but shaking with emotion. It was Jessica, her loyalty to the craft overpowering her allegiance to any individual. She looked around, seeking allies in her stand. "We need justice."

"Justice doesn't pay the bills!" someone countered, the practicalities of life intruding upon ideals. It was an uncomfortable truth, one that resonated with nods from several others. Sapphire had been good for business, no matter the shadows that lingered behind the curtain.

"Nor does it ease a conscience," Nate shot back, unwavering. Amy nodded, her stance resolute beside him, a solid front against the creeping menace of corruption.

Whispers swirled through the group, a storm of indecision brewing. No one wanted to believe that their mentor, their star, could be orchestrating their downfall. But the evidence was there, tangible and damning.

"Where's the loyalty?" Sapphire demanded, his voice cracking under the strain. "After everything..."

"Loyalty to you, or to what's right?" Amy asked, her question slicing through the chaos, bringing a hush upon the room.

Eyes shifted, some down to scuffed shoes, others toward the exit, as if considering escape from the quagmire of deceit. The choice was stark, laid bare in the harsh glow of stage lights.

"Right," someone said at last, the word spoken with resolution. It was Diane again, her gaze now fixed on Sapphire, steely and final.

"Right," echoed another voice, then another, until the murmur became a chorus. The group's foundation shook, cracks widening as loyalties shifted and realigned.

"Enough!" Sapphire bellowed, his control splintering. "You think you can replace me?"

But it wasn't about replacement. It was about truth. And the group, though pained, began inching toward it, step by painstaking step. They were actors, yes, but in this moment, their roles demanded more of them than any script ever could.

"Truth," Martin declared, the lead actor finally taking his cue. "We follow truth now."

Sapphire's hands clenched into fists, the final act playing out not according to his script, but to the unyielding march of justice that Nate and Amy had set into motion.

Chapter 12

Nate's pulse thrummed in his ears, a rhythmic reminder of the tightrope he and Amy were walking. They stood under the probing gaze of Sapphire, whose sharp eyes flickered with the glint of suspicion.

"Something doesn't add up with you two," Sapphire said, her voice slicing through the tense air.

Nate locked eyes with Amy, a silent exchange passing between them. Time to dance on the razor's edge. He adjusted his stance, shoulders squared, as he prepared to parry with words. Survival in this game meant thinking faster, being smarter.

Amy's breath was steady, but her mind raced like a high-speed chase. Every detail of the room sharpened under her scrutiny—the way Sapphire's eyelashes batted a fraction too slow, the imperceptible tightening at the corners of her lips. Amy catalogued each micro-expression, decrypting the unspoken threats.

They had to regain control, and fast. Their mission hinged on maintaining the facade, on staying one step ahead of Sapphire's cunning. Nate's instincts analyzed angles and exits, Amy's tenacity clung to the truth they sought to expose.

Their bond, their shared history of righting wrongs, now thrummed between them—a silent promise to outwit the danger they faced. Nate's mind worked furiously, teasing out strategies, paths to steer the conversation away from the precipice. Amy's focus narrowed, her thoughts laser-etched onto turning the tide.

Together, they stood resolute, a united front against the looming threat of exposure. Nate's empathetic read of human nature, honed in the depths of cyberspace and battlefields alike, paired with Amy's keen eye for detail, formed an unspoken language of survival. In the face of peril, they found strength in each other's resolve, ready to spin a web of deception that would seal their safety—or spell their doom.

Sapphire's eyes narrowed, the dark orbs gleaming with suspicion as he leaned in closer to Nate and Amy. The air seemed to grow thick with tension.

"Darlings, you've been quite the enigmatic duo since you joined our little troupe," Sapphire purred, his voice a velvet threat that belied the sweet moniker. "Pray tell, what's the real reason you're here? Not just for the love of theater, I presume?"

Amy felt her pulse quicken but held Sapphire's gaze with practiced ease. "Sapphire, we've been nothing but devoted to the group," she said, her tone steady and reassuring. "We share a passion for the arts."

"Passion, hmm?" Sapphire's lips curled into a half-smile. "Or is it something... more lucrative?"

Nate interjected smoothly, "We're all here to play our parts, aren't we? Yours just happens to be under the spotlight."

"Indeed," Sapphire snapped back, unamused. "But offstage, it seems you both fancy a bit of role-playing too. Care to enlighten me on your latest characters?"

"Our sex life is nothing of your business," Amy retorted, with a smile. "But isn't imagination the lifeblood of our craft?" she continued, deflecting the insinuation with a hint of irony. "We simply immerse ourselves in the experience."

"Quite the immersive experience, digging through old files backstage, isn't it?" Sapphire countered sharply, the accusation hanging between them like a guillotine blade poised to fall.

"Research for authenticity," Nate replied without missing a beat. "You can appreciate that, can't you? After all, your portrayal of Lady Macbeth was nothing short of haunting."

"Flattery will get you nowhere," Sapphire warned, though a flicker of pride flashed in his eyes before he suppressed it. "I'm watching you two. One false move..."

"Then let's keep dancing, shall we?" Amy offered a smile as disarmingly genuine as she could muster. "After all, the show must go on."

Sapphire's eyes narrowed, a predator scenting weakness. "One false move" he echoed, the words oozing with threat. Nate and Amy stood their ground, a united front against the brewing storm.

"Actually," Nate said, his voice calm but carrying an undercurrent of steel, "We've stumbled upon something during our... 'research.'" He reached into his jacket pocket, the motion slow and deliberate.

The air grew thick with anticipation, members of the theater group leaning in, whispers swirling around the room like leaves caught in a whirlwind. Sapphire's posture stiffened, a statue bracing for impact.

"Behold," Amy declared, her fingers unfurling to reveal a crumpled piece of paper that Nate had placed in her hand. She smoothed it out, holding it up for Sapphire and the rest to see. It was a financial statement, numbers glaringly red, unmistakably implicating Sapphire in embezzlement.

Sapphire's facade cracked, his face draining of color as if someone had pulled a plug, letting the blood seep away from his skin. His mouth opened and closed, a fish gasping on land. The document fluttered in Amy's grasp, a silent testimony to Sapphire's duplicity.

"Impossible..." Sapphire's voice was barely audible over the collective inhale of the crowd. His hands trembled, the air of sophistication peeling away to reveal raw panic. Eyes darted across the sea of faces surrounding him—faces now etched with doubt and betrayal.

He took a step back, as if the evidence had physically struck him, his heel catching on the stage curtain. For a moment, Sapphire teetered, the master of manipulation reduced to a mere mortal losing his balance. His gaze locked with Nate's, searching for a lifeline or a hint of mercy.

But Nate's eyes were resolute, reflecting the truth laid bare before them all. Sapphire had been unmasked, the grand illusion shattered by the cold, hard reality of proof.

Nate leaned in, the corners of his mouth twitching upward. "Not so fast, Sapphire," he said, his voice a low thrum of triumph. He slid another folded paper from his pocket, unfolding it with deliberate slowness. His fingers didn't tremble; they were steady as steel beams.

"Let's take a look at this, shall we?" Amy suggested, her tone laced with the sweetness of victory. She snatched the document and held it high for all to see—a series of emails that painted a damning picture of Sapphire's secret dealings.

The room buzzed with whispers. The performer's eyes widened, the sheen of sweat on his forehead now a beacon of guilt. Sapphire's lips parted, a rehearsed denial dying before it could be born.

"Forgery!" he finally spat out, but the accusation hung limp in the air, unconvincing.

Amy's laugh was like ice cracking. "Nice try. But we both know Nate's too good to leave any trace. Right, darling?"

"Right," Nate confirmed, his nod slow and mocking.

Sapphire's glare flickered between them, a caged animal calculating its next move. He straightened, the slump of defeat banished by a sudden surge of defiance. "You two think you're so clever," he hissed, voice regaining its former strength. "But what about your own secrets? How much did you manipulate to get here?"

A collective intake of breath rippled through the group, eyes darting between the accuser and the accused.

"Go ahead." Nate's challenge was a verbal gauntlet thrown. "Tell them."

"Perhaps I will." Sapphire's words were venomous, aimed to wound. "Maybe they should know about—"

"About what, Sapphire?" Amy cut in, her gaze never wavering. "That we're here to stop you from exploiting this theater for your own gain? That we care about these people more than you ever did?"

Sapphire's mouth snapped shut, the momentum stolen from his sails. He looked around, desperation clawing at his composure as he sought an ally, any ally.

"Or maybe," Nate continued, stepping closer, "they should know how we've been tracking your little escapades for months now. How every move you made only tightened the noose."

"Enough!" Sapphire threw his hands up, a plea dressed as a command. "You have no proof!"

"Actually, we do." Amy waved the emails again, the papers rustling like leaves in a storm. "And there's more where that came from."

They stood their ground, united and unmovable as Sapphire's kingdom crumbled around him.

Sapphire's eyes narrowed, the dark irises burning with a mix of fury and fear. He leaned forward, his voice dropping to a dangerous whisper that seemed louder than any shout could have been. "You think you've won, don't you?"

Nate's posture remained relaxed, a stark contrast to the tension bristling through the room. "It's not about winning, Sapphire. It's about setting things right."

"Pretty words for a pair of meddlers," Sapphire spat back, but Nate noted the tremble in his hand, the slight crack in his polished armor.

Amy's smile held no warmth as she rifled through the papers, her red hair a fiery banner in the dim backstage light. "We're just getting started. How about we talk about the accounts you've siphoned from? Or the promises you broke?"

The drag queen's composure was slipping, his usual grandeur deflating like a punctured balloon. "You wouldn't dare."

"Try us," Amy countered smoothly, her eyes locked on Sapphire, who was beginning to resemble Stanley more with each passing second—less queen, more cornered conman.

Sapphire's next move was sheer desperation, a blade drawn in a verbal duel. "I know people, the kind that would make your lives very unpleasant," he threatened, the menace in his tone unmistakable.

Nate stepped up now, the soldier in him rising to meet the challenge head-on. "And we know evidence, the kind that ends careers—and freedom." His voice solid and unyielding.

"Empty threats," Amy added, her journalistic instinct for truth lending authority to her words.

"Are they?" Sapphire's attempt to sound confident was betrayed by the bead of sweat trickling down his temple.

"Doesn't matter," Nate replied, already calculating Sapphire's next possible moves. "We're not backing down."

"Neither am I," Sapphire hissed, the edge of panic giving way to something darker.

The stand-off continued, neither side yielding, both aware that the next move could be the checkmate.

Nate's hand dipped into his jacket, a practiced motion veiling the tremor of adrenaline. His fingers closed around an envelope, crisp and sealed. "You're so sure of yourself, Sapphire," he said, voice low and steady.

"Because I am," Sapphire retorted, though his eyes flicked to the envelope, curiosity piqued.

"Last chance," Amy warned, her gaze never wavering from the man before them. "Confess, or we go public."

"Bluffing," Sapphire scoffed, but his voice wavered, a telltale crack in his armor.

Amy smirked, exchanging a brief look with Nate. "No bluff." Nate yanked the envelope free and tossed it onto the table between them. It landed with a slap, definitive and accusing.

"Go ahead. Open it," Nate dared.

Sapphire hesitated, then snatched the envelope, tearing it open with a mix of defiance and dread. Papers spilled out, each a damning testament of his deceit—a ledger of embezzled funds, falsified contracts, incriminating emails—all traced back to him, irrefutable.

"Impossible..." Sapphire's face drained of color, his sophisticated facade crumbling like a cliffside in erosion.

"Got you," Amy breathed, satisfaction lacing her tone as she watched the realization dawn in Sapphire's eyes.

"You'll never get away with this," Sapphire hissed, fear flashing through his dark eyes as he scanned the documents. The evidence was undeniable, the paper trail meticulously documented, leading to only one conclusion.

"Already have," Nate replied, standing sentinel over the victory they had secured. "Your move, Stanley."

Sapphire—no, Stanley now—looked cornered, a predator turned prey in the blink of an eye. He scoured their faces for some hint of mercy, finding none.

"Alright," he said, voice barely above a whisper. "You win."

But then, as Nate and Amy exchanged triumphant glances, something shifted. A glint of resolve sparked in Stanley's eyes, the wheels turning behind his calculating gaze.

"Except," he drawled, a sly grin spreading across his face, "you missed one little detail."

"Which is?" Amy challenged, her investigative instinct flaring up.

Stanley leaned back, folding his arms with a newfound confidence that sent a shiver down their spines. "I'm not the mastermind," he said, dropping the bombshell with casual cruelty. "There's someone else—a bigger fish."

Nate's heart hammered, his mind racing. They'd played their hand perfectly, but this revelation hinted at a much larger game. Amy's expression mirrored his own shock, a whirl of questions already forming behind her steely resolve.

"Who?" Nate demanded, the urgency clear in his clipped tone.

Stanley's smile widened, malicious and knowing. "Now, that would be telling."

Chapter 13

The dashboard clock blinked 11:07 PM as Nate drummed on the steering wheel. Their car, a nondescript sedan, idled outside the grand marquee lights of the theater—an ironic beacon of escapism. Exhaustion had hollowed Nate's eyes, and Amy's usually vibrant aura was dimmed by the weight of doubt that now clung to her like a second skin.

"Are we in over our heads?" Nate murmured, his gaze not leaving the illuminated entrance where Sapphire reigned supreme behind velvet curtains. The question hung between them, a specter of their own making.

Amy's hands balled up in her lap, the tension in her knuckles betraying her stoic face. "What if we make it worse, Nate?" Her voice, normally clear and commanding, wavered with uncertainty. "These people—they're not just marks; they're victims, friends. Our friends."

Nate felt the raw edge in her tone, the protective surge that always rose within her when the innocent stood on the precarious edge of collateral damage. He knew the stakes, the tightrope walk between justice and retribution they navigated daily since taking this case.

"If Sapphire smells a rat..." She didn't finish the sentence, but the implication was clear as the fear of unintended consequences shrouded her thoughts. Sapphire's web was intricate, laced with charm and deceit, and they were inches from being ensnared themselves.

"Then we tread carefully," Nate replied, his words clipped yet resolute. He shared her concerns but also knew retreat wasn't in their playbook—not when people's lives and legacies were siphoned away by a man who danced in the spotlight while picking pockets in the shadows.

They sat in silence for a moment longer, their resolve rebuilding amidst the hum of the engine and the distant applause filtering through the theater walls.

Nate's gaze lingered on the rearview mirror, reflecting their haggard faces, the lines of stress etched like a road map of every sleepless night spent chasing shadows. He leaned back, his spine pressing hard against the worn leather, and exhaled a sigh that seemed to carry the weight of their world.

"Is it worth it?" The question hung in the air, loaded with the emotional toll of their mission, the countless hours decoding cryptic trails that led them here, to this moment of doubt. His mind raced with scenarios, each ending with the potential of failing those who had unwittingly become their charge.

Amy shifted beside him, her breaths uneven. "Nate," she began, her voice trembling like a leaf caught in a storm. "What if we can't do this? What if we're not enough to bring Sapphire down?"

The fear in her eyes mirrored his own, a shared dread of failure that gnawed at their resolve. Nate heard the quiver in her tone, felt the tremor of uncertainty that threatened to fracture the foundation they had built together.

"Are we enough, Nate?" Her words were barely above a whisper, but they landed with the force of a gavel, demanding an answer neither was sure they possessed.

The silent, suffocating fog of doubt crept around them, squeezing the car with its cold fingers, forcing them to confront the possibility that justice might slip through their grasp, leaving the theater group exposed to further harm.

Nate's hand broke through the haze of uncertainty, finding Amy's in the dim glow of the car's console. His fingers wrapped around hers, a warm lifeline in the chill of their doubts. He offered her the kind of smile that had once convinced a skeptical jury to believe in impossible innocence—a smile that cut through fear like a beacon.

"Remember Evie?" he said, his voice steady. The woman who had to degrade herself to make ends meet? "We fought for her. We won."

Amy locked onto his gaze, holding on to the memory as if it were a lifeline. "Yes," she whispered, the word a bridge back to stronger days.

"And the kids at the commune," Nate pressed on, his thumb rubbing comforting circles over her knuckles. "We opened locked doors for them and got them to safety."

She felt the movement, a rhythm that pulsed with every victory they'd clawed from the jaws of defeat. Each word from Nate was a beat in a war drum, stirring her heart to battle readiness.

"Can't give up now, Ames." His voice was a command, a call to arms that brooked no argument. "Too much at stake."

Inhaling deeply, Amy drew from that well of shared triumphs, each breath rebuilding her crumbling fortitude. She sat up, spine straight as a mast in stormy seas. Her nod was sharp, decisive.

"No turning back," she agreed, the determination in her eyes igniting a spark that threatened to set the night ablaze. They were warriors in the shadows, guardians of the unprotected.

"Never," Nate affirmed, and in that word lay an oath, a silent pact between them. Together, they would light the way through darkness, relentless in their pursuit of justice.

The engine roared to life, a guttural purr that filled the silence between them. Nate flicked on the headlights, their glow slicing through the theater's cloak of shadows as they pulled away from the curb. The rearview mirror framed the marquee one last time before it disappeared into the night.

"Okay," Nate said, his voice low and steady. "We can't rush this. It's like defusing a bomb."

"Precision over speed," Amy added, her gaze fixed on the dark road ahead. They were navigating more than just streets; they were charting a course through a minefield of morality and danger.

"Exactly." Nate tapped the steering wheel, his mind racing with scenarios. "Sapphire's slick. We need airtight evidence, something that leaves no room for doubt."

"Without putting the group in the spotlight," Amy said. She reached into her bag, fingers brushing against the notepad filled with fragments of their plan. "They're scared, Nate. Embarrassed. They won't come forward, not without a push."

Nate nodded, a silent acknowledgment of the tightrope they walked. Protecting the victims was paramount, but so was ensnaring Sapphire.

"Contacts in law enforcement," Amy suggested, her words crisp as she mentally sifted through their network. "We approach off the record. Guidance, not disclosure. They can help us navigate the legal labyrinth."

"Keep the group out of it," Nate agreed. The suggestion was sound, a way to maneuver within the constraints of the system without triggering alarm bells. They had allies in blue, individuals who shared their disdain for injustice.

"Let's dig deeper first," he said, "before we make our move with the authorities."

Amy nodded, her red hair catching the passing streetlights.

The engine hummed as Nate navigated the neon-lit streets, a labyrinth of shadows and secrets. His jaw set firm, eyes narrowed with purpose.

"Every move counts," Nate said. His instincts flared, every sense attuned to the mission at hand. He could almost hear the click of pieces falling into place, the sequence of moves that would lead them to victory.

"Let's start with what we know," Amy suggested, flipping through pages of notes, each scribble a piece of the puzzle. "Patterns, habits, Sapphire's routines. There's a chink in the armor; we just need to find it."

"Right," Nate acknowledged, eyes reflecting the determination that matched her own. "We stay somewhat covert. Protect the group. No one gets exposed but Sapphire."

"Exactly." Amy's lips curved in a grim smile, the thrill of the chase igniting a fire within her. This was more than a con; it was their crusade.

The car turned a corner, slipping through the city's veins. Silence fell, heavy with unspoken vows. They were a team, two halves of a relentless force. Together, they'd bring Sapphire down.

Nate's fingers flew across the keyboard. Amy, meanwhile, was hunched over her laptop, eyes scanning financial statements, hunting for discrepancies. They had turned their living room into a makeshift command center, papers strewn about, each scribbled note a breadcrumb on the trail leading to Sapphire.

"Here," Amy said, voice taut with focus as she pointed at a series of transactions that didn't add up. "Shell companies feeding back into accounts under different names. It's a classic money laundering pattern."

"Got it," Nate grunted in reply, cross-referencing the data with the aliases they knew Sapphire used. The connections spiderwebbed across the screen, a clear picture emerging from the chaos.

They subsisted on coffee and cold pizza, sleep a distant memory. Nate felt the old anxiety gnawing at his insides, the fear of missing something crucial, of being too late. But he squashed it down, let the soldier in him take control—disciplined, methodical.

Amy rubbed her temples, feeling the weight of their task. Doubt whispered in her ear, but she silenced it with thoughts of the victims, their hopes and dreams exploited by Sapphire's greed. She looked over at Nate, saw the same resolve etched in his features, and it steeled her spine.

"Something's off here," Nate muttered, zooming in on a cluster of IP addresses. They were a maze, but he had learned to navigate these labyrinths. Patterns emerged, a digital signature uniquely Sapphire's. He locked onto it, tracing the digital breadcrumbs back to their source.

"Keep pushing, Nate." Amy's encouragement cut through the haze of fatigue. "We're close."

"Always do," he replied, though his voice was rough with exhaustion. But there was a new energy in his movements; they were honing in on their quarry.

The web of deceit unraveled further, each strand painstakingly mapped until they could see the entire vile tapestry. With every lead they followed, every piece of evidence they logged, Sapphire's downfall seemed more inevitable.

"Can you believe we're actually doing this?" Amy asked during a rare moment of quiet, her voice barely above a whisper.

"Have to," Nate replied without looking up, his gaze still fixed on the screen. "No turning back now."

"Never was," she agreed, her fingers resuming their dance over the keys.

They were two parts of a whole, bound by a shared purpose, fortified by mutual trust. The doubts still came—relentless, nagging—but together, Nate and Amy pressed on, each discovery a testament to their unwavering determination. The truth was out there, and they would drag it into the light, no matter the cost.

Amy leaned over Nate's shoulder, her breath shallow with anticipation as she watched lines of code and encrypted messages spill across the screen. They were on the cusp of something big, something that would end Sapphire's reign of deceit.

"Got it," Nate said, a triumphant edge to his voice. The screen displayed a series of transactions, each meticulously documented, irrefutably linked to Sapphire's alias. It was the smoking gun they needed—proof that Sapphire had been siphoning off the theater group members' savings with the stealth of a seasoned thief.

"Look at this..." Amy traced a line of entries with her finger, her eyes narrowing. "It's obvious identity theft."

"Enough to put him away for a long time," Nate agreed, his pulse quickening with the realization that they had finally cornered their elusive adversary.

They exchanged a look, a silent communication that spoke volumes. This was the culmination of weeks of relentless pursuit, of diving into the murky depths of Sapphire's digital wake. They'd unearthed a trail of exploitation, a calculated betrayal of trust that had left lives in shambles.

"Let's compile everything," Amy said, her voice steady with resolve. She began organizing the files, categorizing the evidence with meticulous care. Nate admired her precision, the way her mind worked with such clarity even under pressure.

Hours passed, the night deepening around them, but they didn't waver in their focus. They compiled documents, cross-referenced accounts, and double-checked every piece of data. When they finally stepped back, it was with the knowledge that they held the power to dismantle Sapphire's charade completely.

Amy let out a long breath, her shoulders relaxing slightly. "We did it, Nate."

"We did," he acknowledged, allowing himself a moment of pride before the weight of their next steps settled upon him.

They sat side by side, bodies weary but spirits fortified by the justice within their grasp. Their reflection in the darkened window pane showed two figures, united in both shadow and purpose. Nate felt the familiar surge of determination, the drive that had propelled him from the military to the world of ethical hacking. Amy's resilience, born from her own quest for truth, mirrored his own.

The road ahead was fraught with challenges. They knew the battle to bring Sapphire to justice would be fought in courtrooms and corridors of power, where the truth could easily be overshadowed by legal maneuvering. But in this quiet space of shared conviction, doubts receded like shadows at dawn.

"Ready for what comes next?" Nate asked, his voice low.

"Always," Amy replied, her hand finding his in the darkness.

Together, they stood, ready to step forward into the light, their bond an unbreakable chain of courage and commitment. The fight for justice awaited, and Nate and Amy Everhart would face it head-on, side by side.

Chapter 14

Nate's jaw clenched as he stepped into the dimly lit dressing room, Amy a shadow at his side. Sapphire lounged before them, the spill of sequins and silk around him failing to conceal the tension in his posture. Nate locked eyes with the drag queen, his gaze sharp as a scalpel.

"Cut the act, Sapphire," Nate said, the words clipped. "We're not blind. Who's helping you pull the strings?"

Sapphire's laugh was rich and false, echoing off the walls adorned with vibrant costumes and wigs. He flicked a perfectly manicured nail against a towering heel, feigning indifference.

"Darlings, whatever do you mean?" Sapphire's voice dripped with condescension. "An accomplice? You've been watching too many spy movies."

Amy's lips curled, the red of her hair almost a warning flare. "Don't play dumb. It doesn't suit you."

"Me? Never," Sapphire purred, but his smile didn't reach his eyes. "You give me too much credit. I'm just a performer, after all."

Nate unfolded a sheaf of papers, the stark white against the dark lacquer of the dressing table. "Let's talk facts, Sapphire," he said, his voice steady, edged with steel.

He slapped down photos of bank statements, printouts of emails, and a list of names—all victims of identity theft. The patterns were there, clear as day, a breadcrumb trail leading to a grand feast of deception.

"Multiple accounts, all drained within days of your little 'performances,'" Amy added, her tone icy, her fingers tracing over the documents. "Each of these people attended your shows. Coincidence? I think not."

Sapphire's painted façade cracked, his eyes darting from the evidence to the only door. He adjusted his wig, a nervous tick betraying the calm he tried to project.

"Patterns can be misleading, darlings," he said, but the quiver in his voice betrayed him.

"Are they?" Nate challenged, stepping closer. "Or perhaps they're the signature of an artist. Your art being thievery."

"Enough people for a class-action lawsuit," Amy mused aloud, though her gaze never left Sapphire. "And enough to pique the interest of federal agents."

Sapphire licked his lips, the taste of fear sour on his tongue. His mind raced for exits, for alibis, for any thread of escape from the tightening web. He laughed, a hollow sound, devoid of humor.

"Federal agents? Now who's spinning tales?" he scoffed, even as his hand slipped unnoticed toward a hidden latch beneath the vanity.

But Nate was watching, always watching. "No tales here. Just the truth—and it's catching up with you."

Nate leaned in, his gaze fixed on Sapphire. "We know it's not just you. Who is it? Who's helping you?"

Sapphire's laugh faltered, the edges of his lips twitching into a grimace. He glanced at the door again, then back to Nate and Amy, trapped by their unrelenting scrutiny.

"Come on, Sapphire," Amy pressed, her voice sharp as a scalpel. "We're not playing audience to your solo act. There's another player sharing this stage."

"Think hard," Nate added, his voice low and steady, "because every second you stall, you dig yourself deeper. And we're not here to throw you a lifeline."

Sapphire's eyes flitted between them, seeking an ally but finding none. The once masterful performer now looked like a cornered animal, his chest rising and falling rapidly.

"Okay, okay!" Sapphire's voice broke, the act crumbling. "It's... it's Martin, alright? Martin's been in on it since the beginning!"

Nate exchanged a glance with Amy, their expressions unreadable, but their thoughts aligned—a mix of vindication and disbelief. Martin, the lead actor, the passionate thespian, was the last person they'd pegged for a thief's accomplice.

"Martin?" Nate's voice was a controlled rumble. "How did he fit into your little scheme?"

Sapphire's shoulders slumped, defeat etched into the lines of his makeup. "He... he had access. To the theater-goers, the patrons... He could get the information we needed quietly."

Amy nodded, taking mental notes, while Nate's mind raced ahead—strategizing their next move. They had the truth. Now they needed justice.

A hush fell over the room, broken only by the distant echo of stagehands dismantling a set. Nate's eyes narrowed, his posture rigid, a soldier scenting battle. Amy's fingers twitched, itching for her notebook, her journalist's instincts on fire.

"Martin?" she echoed, disbelief coloring her tone.

Nate stepped closer, his shadow falling over Sapphire who seemed smaller now, stripped of his grandeur and glitter. "The guy who brings coffee for the crew? Who remembers everyone's birthday?"

"Exactly," Sapphire murmured, a hint of defiance returning to his voice. "He's the perfect front."

Amy's lips parted in shock, but it was the twist yet to unfold that would shove her from surprise deep into the realm of incredulity.

"Where is he?" Nate demanded, his gaze cutting through the layers of deception.

"Backstage," Sapphire replied, resigned. "Probably...fixing something or counting tonight's take."

"Or both," Nate muttered.

They found Martin amid the clutter of costumes and props, his hands fluttering nervously over a sequined dress. The sight of them caused him to start, his eyes darting around like a deer caught in headlights.

"Martin Brown," Nate said, his voice steel wrapped in velvet. "We need a word."

"About what?" Martin asked, feigning innocence.

"Your side gig with Sapphire," Amy cut in, her piercing gaze holding him in place.

Martin's expression faltered, and then, unexpectedly, he laughed—a short, bitter sound. "You got me," he admitted, and there was a tinge of relief in his voice as if a weight had been lifted.

"Didn't think you'd be part of this," Nate said, arms crossed, the betrayal personal.

"Life's full of surprises," Martin retorted, his bravado slipping.

"Care to explain?" Amy prodded.

Martin exhaled, a wry smile touching his lips. "I'm bi, honey." He paused, looking between them. "Sapphire—Stan—he's magnetic. On stage, off stage...it doesn't matter. He, she, satisfies me if you know what I mean."

"Go on," Nate urged, a silent command.

"I flirted with you, Amy, because you're stunning. And I meant it. But with Stan..." Martin's gaze drifted away, lost in a thought he didn't voice out loud.

"Stan as Sapphire," Amy clarified, the pieces slotting together.

"Exactly," Martin affirmed. "And when he's Sapphire, my heart races. He used that, knew I wanted him. It was easy for him to pull me into the scheme."

"Stealing personal information," Nate concluded, disgust plain in his tone.

"Helping him with his little performances," Martin confessed, shoulders hunched. "I got the access, he got the data."

"Quite the double act," Amy said dryly.

"More like a twisted duet," Nate corrected.

Their shock gave way to resolve, the revelation binding them tighter in their quest. Martin, trusted by all, had played them best of all. Now it was their turn to set the stage for justice.

Martin shifted uncomfortably under the scrutinizing gaze of Nate and Amy, his facade cracking. "It's not like I had much choice," he muttered, avoiding eye contact. "Sapphire...Stan, he knew exactly which strings to pull. I was caught up in the rush of it all, the danger, the—"

"Save it, Martin," Nate cut in sharply, his voice a blade slicing through the air.

"Coercion? Or just an excuse for thrill-seeking?" Amy asked, her tone ice-cold. She leaned forward, her eyes probing.

"Thrills don't justify theft," Nate added, stepping closer, crowding Martin's space.

"Look, I'm not proud, okay?" Martin's voice rose, tinged with desperation. "But when Sapphire becomes Stan...or Stan becomes Sapphire...it's intoxicating. He promised moments that—" His voice wavered.

Amy shook her head, unimpressed. "Promises don't clear your record, Martin."

"Stan played me. I was addicted to the attention, the connection," Martin pleaded, searching their faces for a glimmer of sympathy. "You've got to understand, it was more than just physical. It was emotional manipulation."

"Manipulation you willingly danced to," Nate pointed out, his military background shining through in his uncompromising stance.

"Even if that's true," Amy said, folding her arms, "you still chose to break the law."

"Did the thought of the real victims ever cross your mind, Martin?" Nate asked, the ethical hacker within him disgusted by the misuse of personal data.

"Of course, it did," Martin protested weakly. "But by then, I was in too deep. And Sapphire...he has a way of making everything else seem insignificant."

"Except it's not insignificant, is it?" Amy's voice was a scalpel, dissecting his excuses.

"We're not here to play psychotherapist," Nate reminded him. "We have a responsibility—to the people whose lives you helped ruin."

"Responsibility," Martin echoed, a hollow sound as the enormity of his actions settled on his shoulders.

"Right," Nate said, nodding once. "And we're going to make sure you and Sapphire face the consequences."

Amy's eyes met Nate's, a silent agreement passing between them. Martin's confession was just the beginning. Now it was time to untangle the web of lies and deceit, stitch by stitch. The elaborate con was unraveling, and they were the ones holding the thread.

Nate's jaw clenched, the muscles in his neck taut as a bowstring. Amy's eyes narrowed to slits, her breaths shallow and measured. The air in the room grew thick with tension, a tangible force that pressed against their resolve.

"Enough games," Nate snapped, his voice low, a growl of contained fury. "We've danced around your lies for too long."

Sapphire's once-impenetrable facade showed cracks, his laugh lines more like fault lines now. Martin shifted from foot to foot, the actor in him unable to find his mark.

"Think we're fools?" Amy challenged, stepping forward, her investigative instincts flaring. "You two are part of something bigger, and it ends now."

Nate advanced; Sapphire retreated. An unspoken choreography of predator and prey played out in the cramped space. Martin looked between them, a trapped animal in headlights.

"Tell us everything—every dirty detail," Nate demanded, his military precision cutting through the stammered half-truths.

Amy circled, her reporter's gaze dissecting their every micro-expression. "The truth, or we tear it from you," she vowed, her words laced with a promise.

Martin's eyes darted towards Sapphire, then back at the relentless couple. His resolve was crumbling, a sandcastle at high tide. Sapphire's breaths came quicker, the scent of fear mingling with the stale air.

"Alright!" Sapphire burst out, his voice cracking under the strain. "We did it, okay? We did it all!"

"Names," Amy insisted, her pen ready to record the final act of their downfall.

"Contacts, accounts, everything you've got," Nate piled on, his hacker's mind already racing ahead to the next moves.

The confrontation reached its boiling point, the pressure cooker of truth about to explode.

Chapter 15

Nate's gaze swept the empty park before nodding to Amy, their meeting spot shrouded in the comfort of shadows and silence. He checked his watch – they were alone, with only the rustling leaves as witnesses. "We've got to nail this down tight," he murmured, a steely edge sharpening his usual charismatic tone.

Amy, her red hair a stark contrast against the night, nodded in agreement, her eyes reflecting the flame of determination that always seemed to dance within. "They won't be getting away with it," she promised, the words punctuated by the clench of her fist.

"Alright. Let's lay it all out," Nate said, unzipping his backpack to reveal piles of papers, USB drives, and a laptop – the fruits of their investigations. His fingers flew over the keyboard, calling up files and notes, organizing chaos into clarity.

"Start from the top," Amy instructed, leaning over his shoulder, her investigative instincts kicking in. "Every performance date, every incident, we link it back to Sapphire."

"Or Stanley," Nate corrected, his brain already categorizing dates and data points. "He's two-faced in more ways than one." He tapped at the screen, pulling up a spreadsheet. Rows and columns began to fill with information, a digital mosaic of guilt slowly taking shape.

"Here," Amy pointed, her finger hovering above a line of text. "The night of the gala. That's when the first identity theft happened."

"Right on cue," Nate muttered, his brow furrowed as he keyed in the event, drawing a line to the next suspicious activity. Each entry was a breadcrumb leading back to Sapphire, a trail of deception and betrayal.

"Look at this pattern," Amy noted, her quick mind piecing together the puzzle. "Every Sapphire was in town, someone's identity took a hit 2 weeks later."

Nate agreed. "Slips away unnoticed and not around when the crime happens."

"Except he didn't count on us," Amy said with a smirk that carried both pride and promise.

"Got it," Nate announced, a comprehensive timeline spread across the screen. The evidence was there, black on white, irrefutable and damning.

Nate tapped his fingers against the table leg. Amy paced beside him, her fiery hair catching the light with each turn.

"Time to make the call," she said, her voice clipped and decisive. "We have enough."

"Agreed." Nate nodded, his jaw set. They had danced around the edges of legality, but this was bigger than them. Law enforcement had resources they lacked, and Sapphire's game was up.

"Tom Watson," Amy suggested, referring to their seasoned contact on the force. "He owes us one, and he's got the clout to move mountains—or at least, to move a couple of crooks from stage left to behind bars."

Nate pulled out his phone and scrolled through his contacts, stopping on Tom's name. He'd been reliable before, his moral compass pointing steadfast towards justice. A quick conversation later, and the wheels were in motion.

"Let's lay it all out. Every script change, every unauthorized login," Nate said as they spread their collected data across the table. It was a mosaic of malintent; bank statements, emails, backstage whispers all funneling into a portrait of Sapphire and his unwitting accomplice, Martin.

Amy ran her finger along a line of transactions, pausing at the points where Martin's finances intersected with Sapphire's elaborate ruse. "He's clever, I'll give him that," she conceded, though the grudging respect in her tone did not mask her disgust.

"Was clever," Nate corrected, his hands busy compiling the digital evidence into a dossier of deceit. His old hacking skills, once a source of amusement, now served a higher purpose. He felt the familiar rush of adrenaline, the thrill of the chase as zeroes and ones came together to form a net that would snare their prey.

"Here," Amy handed him a stack of papers, her meticulous nature ensuring nothing was overlooked. Receipts for costumes that doubled as receipts for crimes, sign-in sheets that told tales of stolen identities. With every piece they added, the case against Sapphire and Martin solidified.

"Enough here to put them away for a long stretch," Nate murmured, almost to himself. He glanced at Amy, whose eyes burned with the same righteous indignation that always drove them forward.

"Justice for the theater group, at last," she replied, her voice soft but carrying the weight of an unshakable resolve.

They exchanged a look, partners in every sense, their bond forged stronger in the face of adversity. Together, they'd expose the truth, safeguard the innocent, and deliver a final act that Sapphire never saw coming.

Nate's fingers danced across his phone's screen with military precision, tapping out the number that would bridge the gap between vigilante justice and the long arm of the law. Amy hovered at his side in their dimly lit kitchen, her sharp gaze fixed on the glowing rectangle of Nate's phone as it connected.

"Tom? It's Nate Everhart," he said, voice low but clear. "We need to talk. It's about the theater group—there have been identity thefts."

A beat of silence ensued, followed by a grave affirmation from Detective Tom Watson on the other end. Amy's lips tightened into a thin line, anticipation etching creases around her eyes.

"Can you meet?" Nate asked, thumb hovering over the speaker button.

"Sure," came the gruff reply. "The usual spot?"

"Half an hour," Nate confirmed, before ending the call. They shared a nod, silent and succinct. Their plan was set. The next stage awaited.

***

The coffee shop buzzed with the murmurs of mid-morning patrons and the clinking of ceramic on wood. Nate and Amy slipped into the booth opposite Tom Watson, his detective's eyes missing nothing, not even the slight tremble in Amy's otherwise steady hands.

"Thanks for coming, Tom," Amy started, sliding a USB drive across the table with practiced nonchalance. "That's everything—bank statements, emails, surveillance stills."

"Paints a clear picture," Nate interjected, his voice carrying the weight of countless sleepless nights. "Sapphire and Martin—they've been fleecing the group members, skimming identities like it's a sideshow act."

"Got a timeline here," Amy added, tapping a stack of papers methodically arranged in chronological order. Each page was a testament to her journalistic rigor, each bullet point an indictment.

"Good work," Tom grunted, thumbing through the documents with the skepticism of a man who'd seen too many false leads. But as his eyes scanned the evidence, doubt gave way to dawning realization.

"Looks like you two pulled off quite the sting," Tom acknowledged, a hint of begrudging admiration seeping into his tone. He reached for his coffee, sipped, their gazes met with newfound resolve.

***

Nate's fingers curled around a paintbrush, his strokes against the plywood backdrop steady despite the adrenaline coursing through him. Amy, beside him, clipped a faux ivy vine to a trellis with meticulous care. The musty scent of sawdust and paint filled the air of the community theater's backstage, mingling with the tension that crackled like static.

Sapphire paced the stage, his every motion betraying an unease that clawed at the extravagant persona he had crafted. The drag queen's makeup couldn't mask the tightness in his jaw, the way his gaze darted toward the entrance with alarming frequency. Martin, script in hand, rehearsed his lines with a fervor that bordered on desperation, oblivious to the impending storm.

Footsteps echoed from the corridor, a prelude to the climax they'd orchestrated. Detective Tom Watson entered, his presence commanding the room. His eyes locked onto their targets, the embodiment of law in stark contrast to the theatrical chaos.

"Stanley Richards, Martin Brown," Tom's voice boomed, "you're under arrest for identity theft and fraud."

There it was. Straight to the point.

Martin's script slipped from his grasp, fluttering to the ground as he raised his hands in quiet surrender. He knew it was coming. He knew it couldn't last. He knew things were closing in. Sapphire, however, erupted.

"Arrest? This is preposterous! I've done nothing wrong!" His protestations, though loud, couldn't drown out the cold click of handcuffs.

"Save it for the judge," Tom retorted, signaling the uniformed officer who stepped forward to escort the duo out of their fabricated world and into stark reality.

As the door closed behind them, Diane approached Amy, her expression a blend of relief and worry. "What are we going to do now?" she asked, wringing her hands.

Amy turned, her eyes softening. "We'll find someone else for Sapphire's role. The show will go on," she assured, her confidence unwavering.

"And Martin?" Diane's voice held a tremor.

"The rest can cover his parts temporarily. We're a team here," Amy said, placing a comforting hand on Diane's shoulder. "We'll pull together."

Diane nodded, the weight of uncertainty lifting. "Thank you, Amy." Her gratitude was palpable, even as the dust of upheaval settled around them.

Diane exhaled, her shoulders visibly relaxing as she surveyed the half-built set. The scattered hammers and paint cans seemed less chaotic now, less insurmountable. She turned to Amy, a small smile playing on her lips. "Really, I can't thank you enough," she said, the warmth in her tone melting away the remnants of tension.

"Of course, Diane," Amy replied, her voice steady. She scanned the bustling activity around them, her keen eyes missing nothing. Every prop, every costume spoke of potential, of a show that would go on despite adversity. "The group's resilient. They'll shine, especially when the spotlight hits."

Diane chuckled, the sound light and free. "You always had a way with words, Amy. I suppose it comes from sniffing out stories, huh?"

Amy's lips quirked into a knowing grin. "Something like that," she conceded. She watched the theater members adapt to the sudden change, their movements purposeful, their spirits undeterred. It was a testament to their dedication, their passion for the craft.

"Besides," Amy continued, "when you've got a crew this dedicated, not even a curveball like today can stop the show." Her eyes met Diane's, imparting confidence, sharing a silent promise that all would be well.

"Your faith in us means the world," Diane said, clasping Amy's hand for a moment. Gratitude shone in her blue eyes, the motherly concern that had furrowed her brow now smoothed by reassurance.

"Let's make it a performance to remember," Amy declared, squeezing Diane's hand before letting go. She stepped back, allowing herself a moment to appreciate the collective effort. This was more than just a play; it was a community standing strong in the face of deceit.

"Absolutely," Diane agreed, her voice firm with newfound conviction. She glanced once more at the stage, then back at Amy. "With you and Nate on our side, how could we fail?"

Amy gave a nod of acknowledgment, her stance resolute. "You won't," she stated simply. It wasn't just a pledge; it was a fact.

Chapter 16

The rehearsal space buzzed with tension. Theater group members huddled in clusters, their buzz of speculation punctuated by nervous laughter and furtive glances toward the empty stage. They knew the gravity of the meeting; rumors had been swirling, but specifics were elusive.

Nate's boots thudded against the wooden floor as he emerged from the wings, Amy at his side. Their strides were purposeful, each step a silent drumbeat commanding attention. The murmur quieted to a hush as all eyes fixed on them.

"Thank you for coming," Nate began, his voice steady. His dark eyes swept over the familiar faces, each brimming with trust. He could almost feel their collective pulse, racing with the fear of the unknown.

Amy's gaze was equally penetrating, her red hair a flame in the stark lighting. "We've uncovered something important." Her words cut through the silence, sharp and clear.

"About Sapphire and Martin," Nate continued, locking eyes with the group one by one. A practiced scan, picking up on the flickers of anxiety, the tight grips on chair backs. "They've been arrested."

A collective intake of breath filled the room. Nate's disclosure hung heavy, like a storm cloud ready to burst.

"Identity theft," Amy added, the weight of each syllable measured. "Some of you have first hand experience of their antics, but it wasn't limited to members of this group. You are not alone."

Nate watched as the truth sank in, defenses crumbling. He laid out the facts, stark and undeniable. "Bank accounts drained. Credit lines maxed out. All traced back to them."

"Your privacy, your finances, exploited," Amy drove home the point, her scrutiny unwavering. She painted the picture of deceit, a canvas muddied with betrayal.

"Crafty, systematic," Nate said.

A gasp tore through the crowd like a rip in a curtain. Faces blanched, eyes wide as saucers, reflecting the stark fluorescent lights above. Disbelief etched into every furrowed brow and gaping mouth.

Standing amid the storm, Nate and Amy became the eye—the calm, unwavering center. They had lit the fuse, now they watched the firework of emotions display before them.

Then she moved—Diane. Motherly, nurturing Diane. She wove through the chaos, a beacon of warmth in the cold room. Her approach was gentle, yet every step resonated with purpose. Her blonde curls quivered as she stepped forward, blue eyes shimmering not with tears but with something fiercer—gratitude.

"Thank you," she said, voice trembling more with relief than frailty. "Both of you."

Her words were a lifeline thrown into turbulent waters. "Without your dedication..." She paused, composing herself, the strength of her conviction steeling her spine. "We might never have known. You've protected us."

Her gaze held Nate's, then Amy's, passing between them a silent acknowledgment of their shared fight for justice. In her eyes, a reflection of Nate's own commitment—an echo of battles past, a promise of wars yet to come.

"Your courage," Diane continued, "your pursuit of truth... It means everything."

Nate felt the weight of responsibility settle on his shoulders, an old, familiar burden. He met her gratitude with a nod, a silent vow that he and Amy would see this through to the end.

Amy beside him—steady, resolute—was the anchor keeping him grounded. Together, they stood before the group, ready to weather the tempest of righting wrongs and mending broken trusts.

Cynthia rose, her silhouette framed by the clutter of costumes and props behind her. "We need a lawyer," she declared, her voice slicing through the murmurs like the precise cut of her fabric scissors. The glint in her blue eyes was steel, not silk. "They took from us—it's time we take back."

Around her, heads bobbed—marionettes spurred to motion by her conviction. The group huddled closer, their collective shadow swallowing the room's lingering doubt.

"Justice isn't just about punishment," Cynthia continued, hands on her hips as if ready to measure them for battle armor. "It's about restitution. We can't let Sapphire and Martin get away with this."

Nods turned vigorous. Voices rose, interweaving into a tapestry of resolve. They traded names of attorneys like playing cards, each suggestion weighted with hope.

"Whatever it takes," someone said—a mantra repeated, adopted, owned. Their unity was a fortress; the scent of retribution hung thick like stage fog.

"Action," Nate murmured, his pulse quickening to the rhythm of their newfound solidarity. Amy stood beside him, a silent sentinel, her eyes alight with the fire of purpose.

The script had changed. New roles were cast—not victims, but victors, reclaiming their narrative, one legal brief at a time.

Susan Thompson's eyes scanned the room like a hawk, her green gaze piercing through the haze of shock still lingering in the air. She stepped forward, a clipboard already materializing in her hand as if summoned by the gravity of the situation. "I'll coordinate with the lawyer," she declared crisply, her voice cutting through the chatter.

"Documents, statements, evidence," she listed off, each word sharp and decisive. Her brow furrowed, concentrating on the task at hand. The stage manager in her was already cataloging their arsenal for battle—receipts, emails, every scrap that could tip the scales toward justice.

"Every bit helps," she stated, looking around, meeting the eyes of her fellow group members one by one. "We're getting compensation.

We will make them pay." Determination set her jaw firm, a reflection of her resolve not to let their trust be shattered by deceit.

Without missing a beat, Robert Johnson, the man usually behind flamboyant fabrics and striking set pieces, rose to his feet. He leaned against a half-painted backdrop, the image of resilience. "Let's put on a show," he suggested, his brown eyes flickering with the spark of an idea. "A fundraiser."

"Brilliant!" someone exclaimed, and the energy shifted, crackling with possibility.

"Community support," Robert continued with a flourish, "they love us out there. They'll come. They'll donate. They've seen our plays; they'll invest in our plight."

"Justice has a price tag," Susan added dryly, nodding in agreement. But behind the practicality of her words, there was an unspoken camaraderie—a silent acknowledgment of Robert's insight.

"Costumes, props, acts—we have it all," Robert said, gesturing grandly, already envisioning the event.

"Let's turn this tragedy into triumph," he proclaimed, and the room erupted into a chorus of assent, a symphony of solidarity.

"Fundraiser it is," Susan confirmed, scribbling fiercely onto her clipboard. "Now, let's get to work."

Nate leaned back against a cool, shadowed wall, arms folded. Amy stood next to him, her gaze sweeping over the bustling group. A sense of achievement simmered between them, unspoken but shared. They had peeled back the curtain on deceit, and now watched as their revelations stitched the group into a tighter tapestry of camaraderie.

"Can you believe it?" Amy murmured, her voice a low hum of pride.

"Believe it? I expected it," Nate replied with a wry smile, his eyes never leaving the ensemble. "They're fighters."

Across the room, voices rose in a cacophony of planning. Ideas ping-ponged from one member to another, each suggestion met with vigorous nods or thoughtful tilts of the head. Their energy was palpable, a living force that seemed to breathe new life into the rehearsal space.

"Thoughts on the next step?" Amy tilted her head towards Nate, her red hair catching the light like flickers of flame.

"Let them lead. They've got this," he said, his confidence in the group clear.

Nate's military background had instilled in him a sense of strategy and leadership, yet here he stood, content to let others take the helm. His past—a tangled web of codes and covert operations—had taught him the value of stepping back when unity took root.

Amy nodded, understanding. Her own history echoed with battles fought for truth and justice. She knew when to dive into the fray and when to offer support from the sidelines.

As the theater members' plans solidified, a collective momentum built. It swelled within the confines of the room, pushing against the walls with the force of shared purpose. The undercurrent of their determination buzzed through the air, electric.

Finally, Diane turned to Nate and Amy, her eyes glistening with gratitude. "We owe you both so much," she said, her voice thick with emotion. "If not for your courage, we'd still be in the dark."

The rest of the group chimed in, a chorus of thanks echoing Diane's sentiment. They clustered around the couple, faces alight with hope and resolve.

"Hey, we just pulled at the thread," Nate responded, his voice touched by humility. "You all are the ones weaving it back together."

"And we'll continue to do so," Susan interjected, a fierce glint in her eye. "Together."

"Exactly," Amy agreed, her hand finding Nate's. "Together."

The room settled into a charged silence, every person present bound by a common goal. They knew the road ahead would be fraught with challenges, but they faced it united, ready to reclaim what had been taken from them.

"Let's get started," Robert declared, breaking the quiet. "We have a fundraiser to plan. We have justice to serve."

"Let's make it happen," Nate said, nodularityding to each of them with respect.

As the group dispersed, back to their huddle of fervent discussion, Nate and Amy exchanged a look of quiet satisfaction. They had set the stage. Now it was time for the actors to play their parts.

Nate's gaze swept the room, every face a story of resolve. He could feel the pulse of the rehearsal space quicken, as if the walls themselves were bearing witness to a pivotal moment in the theater group's history.

"Checklist," Susan barked out, her stage manager instincts kicking into overdrive. "We'll need receipts, bank statements, emails."

"Got it," Cynthia chimed in, her voice steady despite the swirl of emotions. She was already tapping away on her phone, her fingers swift and sure.

Diane stood by the window, sunlight casting a halo around her motherly silhouette. "We're more than a group now," she murmured, more to herself than anyone else. "We're a family."

Amy shared a knowing look with Nate. She didn't need to speak; their partnership was built on understanding that ran deeper than words.

"Family that fights back," Robert added, his flamboyant flair absent, replaced by a steely determination that matched his precise sketches.

"Exactly," Nate said, nodularityding in agreement. His eyes locked with each member in turn, affirming their unity without the need for grand speeches.

"Can we count on the community for support?" Diane's question floated above the growing hum of strategy.

"Let's tap into the local network, set up crowdfunding," suggested Cynthia, her youth not diminishing the weight of her contribution.

"Good thinking," Nate replied. "Every cent helps."

"Time's not our friend," Susan cut in, her urgency palpable. "We hit this hard, fast."

"Agreed," Amy nodded, her investigative instinct flaring. "No dragging feet."

"Meet here tomorrow, same time," Robert declared. "Bring everything you've got."

"Will do," came the chorus of replies, a symphony of solidarity.

"Rest tonight," Nate advised, his tone firm but caring. "Tomorrow, we hit the ground running."

"Thanks, Nate. Amy." Diane's gratitude was echoed in nods and soft smiles.

"Thank us when we're done," Amy said, her hand squeezing Nate's. "For now, work."

The rehearsal space thrummed with energy as the group dispersed, each person carrying a piece of the collective burden, each heart beating to the rhythm of a common cause. The stage was theirs to command, and they wouldn't yield until the final act was played.

Chapter 17

The stage lights dimmed. The final applause echoed as Nate and Amy stepped into the wings, their hearts pounding in rhythm with the fading ovation. Relief washed over them like a cool breeze on a sweltering day—mission accomplished. They exchanged glances, unspoken words passing between them: they'd done it.

Backstage was a labyrinth of props and costumes, but they navigated it with ease. The scent of sweat and greasepaint lingered in the air—a stark reminder of the roles they'd played, the masks they'd worn. This was more than a performance; it was a con, an elaborate ruse that had just paid off.

"Goodbye and good luck," whispered one of the actors as they passed by, his hand brushing Nate's shoulder. The camaraderie among the troupe had been genuine, a pleasant byproduct of their scheme. Amy smiled at the gesture, her eyes reflecting a hint of melancholy. These friendships were real, even if their reasons for being here weren't.

They stepped outside, the night air crisp against their skin. It was quiet now, away from the theater's hustle—the calm after the storm. They walked side by side down the steps, the old stone cold and solid beneath their feet.

"Did you see their faces?" Nate asked, breaking the silence. "They didn't suspect a thing."

"Of course not," Amy replied, her red hair catching the moonlight. "You were brilliant. You always are." She meant it. His ability to read a room, to weave deception with truth—it was an art form. And she, with her knack for detail, ensured no thread was left untied.

"Couldn't have done it without you," he said, sincerity lacing his voice. He glanced at her, pride swelling in his chest. Together, they'd tilted the scales of justice just a bit more in the right direction.

Amy sighed, a sound that carried layers of fatigue and satisfaction. They'd entered the world of the theater as strangers and emerged as part of its fabric. Bonds had been formed, trust earned. All in service of the greater good, yet leaving behind those connections wasn't easy.

"Those people—" she started, then paused, searching for the right words. "They reminded me why we do this. Why we can't stop."

Nate nodded. This was more than a job. It was a calling—a shared purpose born from past wounds and a desire to protect the innocent. He understood her completely; after all, they were two halves of the same whole, united in heart and cause.

Silent footfalls marked their passage as they left the theater behind, stepping out of the spotlight and into the shadows where they thrived. Ahead lay their sanctuary, their respite, their home. But tonight, they carried with them the echoes of applause and the warmth of newfound kinship.

For Nate and Amy Everhart, the con was over, but the fight for justice was never-ending.

Nate slid behind the wheel, the leather of the driver's seat greeting him like an old friend. Amy settled next to him, her posture relaxed yet alert. The car door shut with a thud that sealed them off from the outside world—a world they had just intricately woven themselves into and out of with the finesse of master weavers.

Ignition. The engine purred to life, a low rumble that resonated with their shared fatigue. No words were spoken; none were needed. Their silence was a comfortable blanket, woven through with threads of victory and sheer mental drain. They sat for a moment, the quiet allowing them to transition from their roles on stage to who they were beneath: Nate and Amy, the con artists with a conscience.

He shifted gears, the car easing forward into the flow of traffic. Streetlights flickered on, casting pools of gold on the dashboard. The city hummed around them, alive with energy that contrasted their own spent reserves. Yet the glow lent a softness to their features, highlighting the subtle signs of triumph etched in the lines of their faces.

Buildings blurred past, each one a silent sentinel to their passage. Headlights danced across the windshield, a symphony of motion that echoed the chaos they'd orchestrated—and controlled—within the theater's walls. They were moving through a familiar landscape now, one far removed from the grand deception they'd left behind.

Amy watched the night slip by, the scenery a backdrop to the cascade of emotions tumbling inside her. Nate kept his eyes fixed ahead, steering them through the concrete maze with practiced ease. Their mission had been a gamble, every move calculated, every scene meticulously rehearsed to manipulate the truth hidden in plain sight.

The city breathed its nocturnal song, a lullaby for the victors in this game of shadows and light. As the car glided through the streets, the weight of what they had accomplished settled over them, a mantle that was equal parts burden and badge of honor. They had exposed the corrupt, protected the vulnerable, all under the guise of performance.

Together, they drove on, partners in this elaborate dance of justice. The city lights continued to cast their warm glow, illuminating the path of two souls undeniably marked by the mission they had chosen to accept. Tonight, they had won. Tomorrow, the battle would continue. But for now, they simply moved through the city, the darkness embracing them as they headed towards the sanctuary of home.

The engine hummed, a soft undertone to their shared silence. Nate's fingers tapped the steering wheel, a rhythmic testament to the adrenaline yet coursing through his veins. He shot a sidelong glance at Amy, her profile bathed in the intermittent glow of passing streetlights. The corners of his mouth lifted ever so slightly.

"Damn proud," he said, voice low, the words slipping out like a conspirator's whisper. "We did good, Ames."

Amy turned, her eyes reflecting the city's pulse, mirrors to the night's victories. She nodded, a simple, graceful acknowledgment. Her lips parted, and gratitude laced her voice, imbuing it with warmth amidst the cool air of the car.

"Those bonds we formed..." she began, her gaze now fixed on the dashboard's shadowy contours. "They were real, even if everything else was smoke and mirrors."

Nate's smile deepened, just for a moment, before his eyes returned to the road ahead. Together they had crafted a masterpiece of deception, but amidst the artifice, authentic connections had taken root. Those were the unexpected trophies from their heist against injustice.

The car's engine died, the night's stillness rushing in to fill the void. Nate killed the headlights. Blackness enveloped their modest two-story home. He stepped out, joints protesting softly, weariness tugging at his muscles. Amy followed, her movements lithe, a silhouette against the suburban backdrop.

Their footsteps crunched on the gravel path. Quiet. Comfortable. Home's scent mingled with cool night air—worn leather and the faintest hint of jasmine from last spring's planting. They lingered on the threshold, breathing it in. A sanctuary they had built together, an oasis amid chaos.

Inside, the door shut with a definitive click. A sound that sealed off the world. Nate flicked on the lamp, soft light spilling across the living room. He watched Amy's shoulders relax, the tension wrought by their latest caper dissipating like smoke.

"Home," he murmured.

"Finally," she replied, the word a sigh more than speech.

They gravitated toward the couch, a well-worn haven of comfort. The cushions accepted their weight, familiar indentations cradling tired bodies. For a heartbeat, or maybe an eternity, they simply existed. Two souls allowing the silence to speak volumes.

Nate's gaze rested on the darkened window, reflection staring back—a man shaped by service and survival. A soldier turned guardian in a digital age. He cataloged this moment, another piece in the puzzle of their lives. Together, they had danced on the edge, spinning falsehoods to unmask truths.

Amy's breath was steady beside him, a metronome of living reassurance. She carried the stories, the whispers of the wronged. Her journalistic instincts now intertwined with their mission. The pen and the keyboard were her weapons; empathy and insight her armor.

They sat, not speaking, not needing to. Their shared resolve hung tangible in the space between them, a vow renewed without words. Tomorrow would come, the fight would rage on, but for tonight, they were two halves of a whole, quietly reflecting on the battles behind and the wars ahead.

Amy leaned forward, her fingers tracing an absent pattern on the coffee table. "You know," she started, a wistful tone threading through her voice, "I'll miss them—the theater folks. The laughs we shared."

Nate's head tilted, acknowledgment in the angle of his chin. His eyes remained locked on the wall, the barren canvas mirroring their brief silence.

"Good people," he agreed, the words low and gruff. Shadows played across his face, cast by the dim light that fought against the encroaching night.

She hummed in response, a sound that filled the room with the echo of memories forged under the guise of performance. "They had no idea what we were really doing."

"Doesn't make the bond any less real." Nate's smile was small, a fleeting tribute to the camaraderie they'd woven into the necessary deception.

Together, they sat back, the couch creaking softly beneath their synchronized movement. Silence enveloped them, thick and potent with the residue of adrenaline and purpose.

In the quiet, Nate's thoughts raced—past cons, future plans—a relentless pursuit of justice. Each scam, each elaborate ruse, was a step toward righting another wrong. The mental list of targets never seemed to dwindle, but tonight, there was solace in knowing they'd struck a blow against corruption.

Amy's gaze found his, and in her eyes, he saw the reflection of his own resolve. They understood the stakes, the risks. The impact of their work wasn't measured in gratitude or accolades; it was the silent victory of lives quietly saved from ruin.

The clock ticked on, indifferent to the gravity of their mission. But for this moment, as the world outside their door rushed onward, Nate and Amy paused to acknowledge the difference they'd made—a difference felt not in the roar of triumph but in the whisper of change.

Nate stood first, stretching limbs weary from the night's charade. His motions were methodical, a soldier's discipline veiling the fatigue. Amy watched him for a moment, her investigative eye noting the subtle tension in his shoulders—the price of their relentless pursuit.

"Let's call it a day," she said, her words clipped yet warm.

In silence, they ascended the staircase, a familiar dance of two shadows against the soft glow from the stairwell light. The bedroom door creaked open, a mundane sound that signaled the end of one act and the beginning of another—private, introspective.

Amy's fingers worked through the knots of her fiery hair, each stroke a reflection on the faces they'd encountered—the allies made within the theater group. Nate watched from the mirror, his dark eyes tracing her movements. Theirs was a partnership forged in adversity, solidified by shared purpose.

"Those people... they're good folks," Nate murmured as he unbuttoned his shirt, each pop of fabric a nod to the bonds they had formed, connections not easily dismissed even under the veil of deception.

"More than we could've hoped for," Amy agreed, placing her brush down. Her voice held a tinge of loss, for the roles they'd shed, the personas they'd abandon as they moved on.

With the day's costume discarded, Nate sat on the edge of the bed, muscles relaxing. Amy joined him, her presence a silent echo of gratitude for the friendships they cherished, no matter how fleeting.

"Tomorrow, back to the grind?" Amy asked, her tone somewhere between inquiry and inevitability.

"Tomorrow," Nate confirmed, his reply firm, succinct. Injustices waited beyond their walls, a siren call to those with the skill to answer.

"Tonight, though..." Amy trailed off, leaning into him, seeking the solace offered in the curve of his arm.

"Tonight, we rest," Nate finished for her, an affirmation spoken like a vow.

They lay back, allowing the mattress to accept their weight, their bodies sinking into the familiar comfort of shared resolve. For all the chaos they courted, this was their haven, their respite in a world fraught with shadows.

As sleep beckoned, the room's stillness wrapped around them—a cloak of reprieve, however brief. Tomorrow's battles loomed, but tonight, the war was worlds away.

The world outside faded, replaced by the slow cadence of two hearts in sync. Nate's breathing deepened, each exhale a release of tension. Darkness encroached, not as an enemy but as an ally, granting them the anonymity they often craved.

Sleep was fleeting—a luxury seldom indulged—but tonight, it was theirs to claim. The bed creaked quietly as Nate shifted, his arm still cradling Amy, her head nestled against his chest. There was comfort in the rhythm of their silent communication, words unnecessary in the sanctity of their shared space.

Amy's breathing matched his, the rise and fall of her chest a soothing counterpoint to the thoughts that raced behind Nate's closed eyes. He listened, deciphered the pattern, found reassurance in its predictability. Here, in this room, they were just two souls intertwined, not pawns on the chessboard of criminal enterprise.

Nate's mind wandered, touching upon the morrow's mysteries with the deftness of a seasoned spy. Each new day brought its web of corruption, a new sequence to decode, fresh adversaries lurking in the shadows. Yet these prospects did not quicken his pulse; instead, they fueled the resolve that simmered beneath his calm exterior.

The city's heartbeat pulsed against their windowpane, a reminder of the lives they fought to protect. Each throb a whisper of the silent cries for justice. They were the unsung guardians, cloaked in the guise of ordinary citizens by day, architects of elaborate cons by night.

In the quiet stillness of their bedroom, strategies formed and dissolved. Nate's mind, ever the tactician, already sketched the outlines of their next move. The game was perpetual, the stakes high. But now, folded within the solace of their sanctuary, the urgency of their mission paused—breathed—in tandem with their slumbering forms.

Home. It was more than a refuge; it was the reset button pressed at the end of every caper, the place where Nate Everhart—the man, the protector—could simply be.

Tomorrow beckoned with its siren song of adventure, of risk and exhilaration. But for tonight, in the fortress of their making, Nate and Amy rested. Recuperated. Readied themselves for the dawn of another battle against the underbelly of society.

And rest they did, knowing that when the sun breached the horizon, their minds and bodies would be fortified, prepared to face whatever twisted fate the world had in store. Because for Nate and Amy Everhart, the fight never truly ended—it merely awaited the break of day.

Chapter 18

Nate and Amy sat side by side, swallowed in the plush embrace of their well-worn sofa. A shaft of evening sun sliced through the blinds, painting stripes of gold across their faces. Silence hung between them, not heavy, but filled with the weight of unspoken thoughts.

"Look at us," Nate murmured, his gaze fixed on the crimson hue that danced on Amy's hair, setting it ablaze with light. "Who would've thought we'd end up here?"

Amy leaned into him, her shoulder brushing against his as she followed his gaze out the window. The city's hustle was a faint murmur compared to the pounding of their hearts. "We've come a long way," she agreed, her voice a mix of pride and wonder.

"From shadows to sunlight," he added, the corner of his mouth twitching upwards.

The chuckle that escaped Amy was soft, almost melodic. She turned to face him, green eyes locking onto his. "In the theater, you know, I learned something crucial." Her words flowed with earnest warmth.

"Yeah?" He tilted his head, inviting her to reveal more.

"Trust," she said, nodding slightly. "There were moments, Nate...moments when I had to shut out everything else. Doubts, fears—it was all noise. I had to tune into the scene, the character, the moment."

"Instincts over logic?"

"Exactly." Amy's fingers traced the back of his hand absentmindedly. "You can't fake trust. It's either there, or it isn't. And when the lights hit you, and the audience fades into darkness, you have to lean on it, hard."

"Like we do," Nate whispered, squeezing her hand gently.

"Like we do," she echoed, her smile unwavering even as her mind raced back to those tense scenes on stage, disguised truths woven into every line.

"Couldn't have pulled off any of this without that trust," he concluded, his voice laced with a respect that only deepened their bond.

"Or without each other," Amy added, her heart swelling with the shared victories and close calls that had defined their journey.

The sun dipped lower, shadows stretching across the room, but the glow between them remained untouched—steady, unyielding, and full of promise for the battles yet to come.

Nate leaned back, the leather of the couch creaking under his weight. The room's warmth seemed to soak into his skin as he watched the sun's last rays dance across Amy's fiery hair. He folded his arms, a contented sigh breaking free.

"Remember Diane?" Nate grinned faintly. "She's got this way of making you feel like family—no judgments, just open arms."

Amy nodded, her eyes reflecting a softness reserved for those cherished memories. "Martin, too. His passion's contagious—even when he's offstage."

"Then there's Cynthia," he continued, amusement flickering in his gaze. "Her optimism could light up Broadway. Taught me something about hope."

"And Susan," Amy chimed in, a chuckle escaping her lips, "her precision kept us on our toes. Always one step ahead."

"Can't forget Robert." Nate gestured with an airy hand. "For all his gossip, guy's got insight like no other."

"Friends," Amy mused. "Unexpected but true."

"More than that." Nate's tone grew serious, and he locked eyes with her. "Allies. When push comes to shove, they stood tall. That's not just friendship; it's a battle line drawn in solidarity."

"Battle lines..." Amy whispered, her smile fading into contemplation.

"Speaking of battles..." Nate's eyes darkened, a shadow of regret passing over his features. "We've paid our dues, haven't we? Sacrifices."

"Too many to count." Amy leaned into him, her voice tinged with the weight of their past. "Late nights turned to early mornings, secrets piling up like debts."

"Missed birthdays, anniversaries," he added, the words tasting bitter. "All for the greater good."

"Emotionally battered, sometimes broken," she admitted, leaning her head against his shoulder. "But we pieced each other back together. Every time."

"Because that's what it takes." Nate's jaw set firm, determination etching deep lines around his mouth. "To tear down corruption, expose the lies. For justice."

"Justice," Amy echoed, her resolve hardening like steel. "For every life entangled in their web."

"Every sacrifice," Nate affirmed, his hand finding hers, "worth it."

"Always." Her grip tightened, a silent promise passing between them. "Together."

The room dimmed as the sun surrendered to night, but the resolve within them burned brighter than ever. They were ready, a united front against the darkness that awaited.

Amy paced the length of the living room, her steps deliberate, each one a silent testament to their unwavering mission. She stopped by the window, hands clasped behind her back, and gazed out at the city's silhouette against the twilight sky. The buildings, mere shadows now, stood as guardians of countless untold stories – some of which she and Nate had pried into the light.

"Truth," she murmured, turning to face Nate with eyes that matched the intensity of her convictions. "In a world brimming with deception, it wields power unlike any other."

Nate watched her, his posture relaxed yet alert. He had seen this fire in her before; it was what had drawn him to her from the start. Her passion for justice wasn't just a fleeting sentiment—it was etched into her very being.

"Gratitude isn't a big enough word, Nate," Amy continued, her voice steady and clear. "We've been given this chance, this incredible chance to shield the innocent, to unravel the lies... It's more than a job. It's a calling."

She walked over to where he sat and perched on the armrest beside him, her hand finding his shoulder. "Every step we've taken has led us here, reaffirming my belief that what we do—seeking the truth, fighting for justice—it's vital. Without it, the darkness wins."

Nate nodded, absorbing her words. They resonated deep within him, reinforcing the purpose that had first set him on this path. He looked up at her, his own resolve mirroring hers, but with a hint of weariness lurking beneath the surface.

"Corruption," he said, the word slicing through the quiet room. "It's like a hydra, you cut off one head, two more grow back. We've learned that the hard way."

He stood up, joining Amy at the window. Together they watched the city, its heartbeat pulsing with secrets and scandals they had yet to uncover. "The exploitation we've seen..." Nate's voice trailed off, his mind racing through the web of deceit they'd traversed.

"More battles ahead," he stated, not as a question, but a stark reality. "This community," he gestured vaguely toward the darkening streets, "it's rife with it. People using power to crush the powerless, lining their pockets while others suffer."

Amy squeezed his hand, a silent vow shared between them. "We're not done," she said firmly. "Not by a long shot. There's more out there, waiting for us to dig it up, bring it into the light."

"Then we keep fighting," Nate affirmed, his eyes reflecting a steely determination. "For truth, for justice. For those who can't fight for themselves."

They stood side by side, silhouetted against the window, partners not only in life but in an ongoing war against the shadows. As night descended on the city, their resolve stood as a beacon of hope amid the encroaching darkness.

Nate paced the room, a caged lion with a detective's mind. The last of the sunlight fought through the blinds, throwing stripes across his furrowed brow. "Values," he muttered, more to himself than to Amy. "They're what we've got when everything else is stripped away."

Amy watched him from the couch, her red hair a fiery contrast to the dimming room. "Our compass," she agreed, her voice steady as a heartbeat. "Especially when the storm hits." She thought of the lies they'd untangled, the masks they'd peeled from deceitful faces.

"Tested, yes," Nate said, stopping in front of her. "But never broken." His eyes locked on hers, a silent pact that no adversity could shatter their resolve.

"Every choice we made," Amy started, leaning forward, "it was a stone thrown against Sapphire's glass house." She pictured the theater group members, faces worn by betrayal and hope intertwined. "We aimed to shatter it, to free them."

"Did we?" Nate asked, the question hanging like a challenge.

"Closure, relief," Amy said, conviction coloring her words. "That's what we fought for." Her mind replayed the moments of truth revealed on stage, under the spotlight, where secrets had nowhere to hide.

"Then we did good," Nate concluded, a rare smile breaking through. "We gave them a fighting chance." He reached out, his hand finding Amy's. Together, they were a force, an unbreakable bond forged in the fires of their mission.

"Good," Amy echoed, squeezing his hand. "And we'll keep doing it." They stood united, two silhouettes ready to cast light into the darkest corners of their world.

Nate paced the room, hands clasped behind his back as if marshaling his thoughts into an orderly formation. "Sapphire was just the tip of the iceberg, Amy," he said, his voice carrying the weight of unspoken challenges.

"Like a weed," Amy agreed, her fingers drumming on the tabletop. "Pull one out, and ten more could sprout in its place." She knew the cycle of corruption all too well from her days chasing stories that others preferred stay buried.

"Exactly." Nate stopped pacing and faced her, the setting sun casting long shadows across the floorboards. "We've got to keep digging, exposing every dirty secret until there's nowhere left to hide."

Amy nodded, her red hair catching the last rays of light. "Our work has barely scratched the surface." The thrill of the chase surged within her. It was addictive, this hunt for justice, and she found herself craving the next puzzle to piece together.

"Every con we've pulled, every lie we've uncovered..." Nate's eyes met hers, intense and unyielding. "It's made us sharper, more resilient." His time in the military had honed his strategy skills, but this—this was a different kind of warfare.

"Stronger, too," Amy added. Their partnership had become a well-oiled machine, each playing their part with precision. Her background in investigative journalism gave her an edge in sniffing out leads, while Nate's hacking abilities ensured they stayed one step ahead.

"Going forward, we can't let our guard down, not even for a moment," Nate continued, the urgency in his voice mirroring the stakes they faced. "There are more Sapphires out there, and we owe it to the innocent to bring them to light."

"Agreed." Amy pushed herself out of her chair, resolve steeling her features. "We adapt, we evolve. Every con teaches us something new about the enemy—and ourselves."

"Never stagnant," Nate affirmed, extending his hand toward her. "Always learning."

"Always fighting," Amy finished, slipping her hand into his. Their grip was firm, symbolic of their shared dedication, their intertwined fates. They were two parts of a whole, united by purpose and bound by trust.

The room fell silent around them as they stood together, ready to face the uncertain future. But uncertainty bred opportunity, and Nate and Amy Everhart lived for the chance to tip the scales in favor of justice.

Nate paced to the window, the sun's dying embers painting his profile in hues of determination. Amy watched him, her gaze tracing the familiar lines of his face, the shadows dancing as day surrendered to night.

"Quite a ride," she murmured, breaking the hush that had settled between them.

He turned, eyes locking with hers. "Wouldn't have it any other way." The corners of his lips twitched upward. "Especially not without you."

She rose, joining him at the window, their reflections merged in the glass. "We've come a long way, Nate." Her voice was a soft echo of the strength they both felt. "I couldn't have done this without your guts, your brain... your heart."

"And I without your eye for detail, your quick wit." His hand found hers, their fingers intertwining naturally. "You've got this uncanny ability to see the truth in a sea of lies."

They stood together, silent, absorbing the weight of their shared experiences. A bond forged in adversity, unbreakable and resolute.

As the last light of day slipped away, Nate's gaze hardened with resolve. "It's more than just us now, Amy. We've set something in motion—a force for good. Can't let up."

"Agreed." Amy's voice was steady, her silhouette firm against the encroaching darkness. "We stand for those who can't stand for themselves. For trust. For friendship." She squeezed his hand. "For justice."

"Then it's settled." Nate's words were a vow, spoken into the twilight of their living room but meant for the world beyond. "We keep fighting. We hold tight to what we know is right. And we do it together."

"Always together," Amy affirmed, her stance echoing his unwavering commitment. They remained there, united, as dusk embraced their home, their pact sealed in the quiet strength of partnership.

The room settled into silence, a testament to the pact just made. Shadows stretched across the walls, mingling with the fading light as Nate and Amy sat motionless, each lost in their own thoughts. The world outside their window transitioned from twilight to darkness, mirroring the uncertain landscape they were about to navigate.

Nate's mind raced, yet his body was still. Images of past cons, close calls, and daring escapes flickered like an old film reel. He felt the weight of every decision, every risk taken. His fingers tapped lightly against the armrest, a silent drumming that echoed the steady beat of determination in his chest.

Amy, her profile etched in the dim light, was a statue of contemplation. She replayed the moments of trust built and tested, the quick decisions under pressure that had become second nature. Her eyes, fixed on a point beyond the walls of their safe haven, were sharp, vigilant. They had seen through deceptions and illusions; now they looked ahead to the unseen challenges of their uncharted path.

The air between them was charged with the electric sense of purpose that had always driven them. It hummed with the silent promise of battles yet to be fought, with the knowledge that they were instruments of change in a world rife with shadows.

They knew the road ahead was lined with pitfalls and snares, but it was a road they would tread together. Their journey had honed them, sharpened their resolve. They were a team - seamless, dynamic, indomitable.

As the last vestige of daylight surrendered to night, Nate and Amy's shared silence was a powerful affirmation. No words needed to be spoken; their bond spoke volumes. They rose as one, a united front ready to step back into the fray, their conviction a beacon cutting through the encroaching dark.

Tomorrow would bring new foes, fresh schemes to unravel, more innocents to protect. Nate and Amy would be there, relentless, unwavering. For justice, for truth, for the good fight that never ends.

More?

CheckMate

In the heart of the city, a vulnerable soul is exploited by a powerful tycoon. But when a husband and wife team takes up the fight for

---

1. https://books2read.com/b/bwQLj9

2.   https://books2read.com/u/bwQLj9

justice, they embark on an elaborate and risky mission to extract money from the tycoon and right the wrongs committed.

With their impeccable reputation as high-profile consultants, they cunningly position themselves as experts in the tycoon's interests and values. Orchestrating a meeting that captivates his attention, they unveil an irresistible offer that seems to align perfectly with his ambitions. As the stakes rise, they skillfully tap into his fear of missing out and desire for greatness, gradually escalating the investment with promises of astronomical returns and exclusive perks.

But this elaborate con isn't just about money. The husband and wife team's ultimate goal is to expose the tycoon's exploitation and demand restitution for the victim. With undeniable evidence in their hands, they confront the tycoon, threatening to expose him publicly and unleash legal and reputational consequences.

As the tycoon faces the potential ruin of his empire and confronts his own moral compass, he undergoes a transformation. But can the husband and wife team trust him to fulfill his promises? With every twist and turn, they must stay one step ahead of the tycoon and navigate a treacherous path to justice.

Will the husband and wife team succeed in their mission and bring justice to the victim? Or will their plan crumble, leaving them with regrets and the tycoon unscathed? Discover the truth in this gripping tale of revenge, redemption, and the pursuit of justice.

***

The Great Escape

https://books2read.com/u/bPzqXx[3]

---

3. https://books2read.com/u/bPzqXx

In a world where justice is elusive, Nate and Amy emerge as an unstoppable force against the dark forces of human trafficking. Nate, an ex-military white-hat hacker, and Amy, a fearless investigative journalist, join forces to form a modern-day A-Team.

Their latest mission takes them deep into the heart of a religious commune, where young girls are held captive under the guise of

---

4.   https://books2read.com/u/bPzqXx

spirituality. With the cult leader using twisted interpretations of the Bible to justify his heinous acts, Nate and Amy must infiltrate the operation and expose the truth.

They gain the trust of the cult leader and unravel the intricate web of his trafficking ring. But as they dig deeper, they discover that this is just the tip of the iceberg, with a larger operation lurking in the shadows.

Armed with intelligence and cunning, Nate and Amy race against time to dismantle the operation and save as many lives as possible. There are no guns in this battle, only the power of their minds and unwavering determination.

This action-packed thriller takes readers on a heart-stopping journey through the depths of human trafficking. With every page, they witness the atrocities and feel the adrenaline-fueled pursuit of justice.

With a gripping climax that will leave readers breathless, this novel is a testament to the resilience of the human spirit and the unwavering fight against injustice. A must-read for those seeking a thrilling and morally charged adventure.

Acknowledgements

You.

First and foremost, I would like to express my heartfelt gratitude for choosing to embark on this journey with me. Your decision to purchase this book means the world to me, and I am truly honored to have you as a reader.

Writing this book has been an incredible labor of love, filled with numerous late nights, countless cups of coffee, and unyielding determination. However, it is your presence here that gives my words purpose and breathes life into the pages.

I humbly ask for a moment of your time to share your thoughts and experiences with this book. If you found solace within its pages, if it made you smile, laugh, or shed a tear, please consider leaving a review. Your feedback is invaluable, not only to me but also to other potential readers who may be searching for their next read.

Your review, whether it be a few heartfelt words or a detailed analysis, has the power to influence others and guide them towards this world I have created. By sharing your thoughts, you are not only supporting my work but also helping to create a community of readers who can connect and engage with one another.

I understand that time is precious, and writing a review may seem like a small task in the grand scheme of things. However, I assure you that your words have the ability to make a significant impact, allowing this book to reach even greater heights and touch the lives of more readers.

Once again, thank you for your trust and for joining me on this adventure. Your support means everything to me, and I am forever grateful.

With deepest appreciation,

- Shane

Andy

I've known Andy for more than a decade. We used to work together and he lives a short walk away from me, which is handy for dog walks. Andy is inscrutably honest and a great person to brainstorm plot ideas with. Andy helped with the plot for this book, both introducing questions and answering them. Without him, this book wouldn't exist.

Alison

Alison is one of the coolest people I know. She is humble and plays bass guitar, apparently thinking that's normal and not realising how cool it is. Alison told me that having a book published is a major achievement, somehow not knowing how agog I am when I hear her play.